Walking
Through
The **Pain**

Dean Alleyne

WALKING THROUGH THE PAIN
Copyright © 2017 by Dean Alleyne

Library of Congress Control Number: 2016938323
ISBN-13: Paperback: 978-1-68256-678-7
        PDF: 978-1-68256-679-4
        ePub: 978-1-68256-680-0
        Kindle: 978-1-68256-681-7

All rights reserved. No part of this publication may be reproduced, distributed, or transmitted in any form or by any means, including photocopying, recording, or other electronic or mechanical methods, without the prior written permission of the publisher or author, except in the case of brief quotations embodied in critical reviews and certain other noncommercial uses permitted by copyright law.

Although every precaution has been taken to verify the accuracy of the information contained herein, the author and publisher assume no responsibility for any errors or omissions. No liability is assumed for damages that may result from the use of information contained within.

Printed in the United States of America

LitFire LLC
1-800-511-9787
www.litfirepublishing.com
order@litfirepublishing.com

Contents

Review vii

1	How It Must Have Broken Her Heart!	1
2	Off To School	9
3	Sundays At The Redmans'	17
4	Who Are These People?	25
5	A Mother's Love	33
6	Double Disaster	43
7	Horrifying Days At My Second School	55
8	Mum Hits Rock Bottom	63
9	The Long Road Back	69
10	Scary Moments	79
11	A New Dawning	89
12	A Baptism Of Fire	95
13	Oh, How They Toiled And Struggled!	101
14	Adapting To Village Life	109
15	Under Attack By A Swarm Of Bees	119
16	Fun At The Seaside	125
17	The Young Budding Entrepreneur	135

18	Off To Secondary School	145
19	A Denied Opportunity	161
20	Tenacity Of Purpose	169
21	My Brother Comes To The Rescue	175
22	Boys Will Be Boys	185
23	Leader Of The Pack	189
24	The World Of Work	195
25	Getting To Grips With Primary-School Teaching	205
26	Distant Horizons	217

*To my brother Elliott
who was always there when
I needed a helping hand.*

Persistence is to Success what Carbon is to Steel

Review

Walking through the Pain is a beautiful and extraordinary book and a marvel of humane, sorrowful and lucid observations. Everything about "Walking Through the Pain" is smart - smart characters, smart writing and a smart pace that keeps you reading long after you'd meant to turn out the lights. An original author who gives us a sharp, sobering, mesmerizing account and understanding of the historical background of colonial Barbados. Revealed is a fauvist landscape of primary colours, painted buses, bright calico school uniforms and exotic fruits. The author is blessed with the acutest of antennae and displays genuine talent. The book is touching, gritty, tough, startling, heartfelt, highly detailed and sentimental. A polished and assured prose with isolated parts of a larger vastness, clear images and characters you care about.

Maxine Williams, author of Inside the Burning Tower.: ...

1

How It Must Have Broken Her Heart!

*H*igh up on a ridge in Barbados, stands the little village of St Simons. From here the land dips gently east, west and north to form the valleys of two streams which make their way sluggishly to the Atlantic on the east except during the rainy season when the force of flood water can often remove bridges. To the south, the ridge rises sharply into densely-wooded slopes to form Turners Hall Wood, a fifty-acre patch of tropical forest, the remnants of what was here when the island was first settled in 1627. Still to be seen are samples of Sand Box, Silk Cotton, Fustic, Cabbage Palm, Trumpet Tree, Locust and Macaw Palm for, at just over 700 hundred feet, it captures any rain driven in from the east by the Trade Winds thus creating perfect conditions for dense tropical growth.

Below this wooded slope and stretching out along the ridge was a collection of small chattel houses all standing on posts and blocks of coral limestone. Most of them were strung out on both sides of the main road while others huddled together in isolated pockets some distance away and only accessible by dirt tracks. The one thing common to most of them was a small adjoining galvanized shed, the kitchen from which various aromas of

Caribbean cuisine were wafted on the wind at appropriate times of the day. The village church (Anglican) and the village school stood on two hillocks about 400 yards apart. The flatter area between was the centre to which villagers gravitated to do weekly shopping at the two small shops or to meet friends and have a drink in the bar on Saturdays.

Unlike some of the other families who travelled as much as three-quarters of a mile to get to a shop, the Atkins lived less than thirty yards away from the nearest shop owned by Sidney and Irene Redman who had become very good friends of Stanley and Alice Atkins their neighbours. Sidney was of average build though slightly shorter than Stanley who was tall and slender. With his build, lighter skin and deportment, Sidney was deemed a very handsome man. He had a Jewish father, a trait that manifested itself through his business acumen and his liking for salt beef. In fact, there was a time when his was the only shop in Speightstown where salt beef sandwiches could be bought. Irene his wife was shorter, very attractive and a good conversationalist. Her father drove one of the trams that once connected the suburbs of Bridgetown to the town centre. She saw herself as playing a support role in helping to drive the family business forward. It was a good combination except that, for some reason, they could not have any children and, although they saw it as the thing to complete their marriage, they had grown to accept it.

It was mid-afternoon and the scorching heat of a tropical sun was driving everyone to seek shade. Old men were either sitting in their doorways nodding or in small groups of two or three under a tree taking advantage of any breeze that happened to pass their way. Any conversation that took place was frequently interrupted by intermittent dozes as they would all seem to be under the sleepy narcotic influence of the fruit of the Lotus tree which, according to legend, is believed to cause drowsiness when eaten. These were the conditions that drove Sidney and Stanley to sit near an east window and enjoy a cool breeze gliding up the valley. Stanley took a small towel from his pocket and mopped his wet brow for he had been working all morning in one of his plots of land nearby. Just then the tranquillity of the afternoon was disturbed by the heavy whining of a truck on its way to the sugar factory with a load of cane on top of which sat the two loaders, their shirts soaked through with perspiration. Sidney and Stanley returned a wave to the two men as they disappeared in the distance.

"How much do you think we will get for a ton of cane this year Sidney?" It was the type of question around which many conversations would be held among small farmers at this time of the year. Crop time had just started, a time when the ripe sugar cane on small peasant holdings and large plantations is harvested to feed the hungry crushing mills of sugar factories. Sidney adjusted his seat and cleared his throat.

"Perhaps very little more than you got last year," he replied apprehensively and sharing Stanley's concern for, although not a small farmer himself, he had a very good understanding of the commodity market. It was a significant question for at that time most families in the village either owned or rented a small patch of land on which they grew sugar cane as a commercial crop and short crops like peas, beans, cassava, potatoes and okras for the kitchen. It was the annual income from sugar cane that provided funds with which to build or add to a house, purchase clothes, furniture and much more or even to pay off any small debts they might have accrued during the year.

That afternoon it was a tranquillity only occasionally interrupted by the bark of a dog or the distant moo of a cow sitting under a tree chewing its cud. It was the kind of siesta-time heat that seemed bent on turning everything, animate and inanimate to jelly when Alice Atkins, now very heavy, managed to drag herself with great difficulty up three coral limestone blocks into the shop. She did not have the glow of an expectant mother. Instead anguish, worry and despair were inscribed on her face now almost bathed in perspiration under a slightly worn out straw hat as she wiped a strand of long dark hair from her forehead. She was the first of thirteen children born to Nathan a descendant of Scottish ancestors and Elizabeth of African, Ghanaian to be more precise. Being the first, Alice was overburden with daily chores which was why she welcomed the offer of marriage from Stanley even at an early age.

Her small eyes met Sidney's immediately gripping his attention and driving him to reflect on information culled from conversations between Alice and Irene. He thought of the heartache she had endured every time she lost a baby and of that motherly instinct driving her to replace each one, only to have her expectations dashed by a 'still-birth' or a loss within six weeks of birth. She had already suffered five consecutive loses previous to the one she was currently carrying. He thought of her feeling of emptiness and failure as well as the abiding fear of losing this one even before it was two months old, but it also brought sharply into focus the inability of his wife Irene to have children and what he might be able to do to help both parties.

Sidney saw this moment as too good an opportunity to be missed. He squinted short-sightedly into Alice's face who managed a wobbly smile while leaning against the counter breathing heavily, and then gazed at Stanley. The scene in front of Sidney tugged at the very core of his heart to set his thoughts racing. *"This is our lucky day. It is a chance not to be missed. I am going to do something I always wanted to do, something that would satisfy our needs and theirs."* He swatted an annoying fly from his face and glanced at Stanley again for a few moments before rising slowly with the look of someone who had just made a major decision and made his way to serve Alice still leaning against the counter for support. He levelled his eyes with hers. "Alice, I want that baby when it's born and I don't care if it's a boy or girl," he exclaimed and sounded concern. She was touched and remained silent for a long moment searching for the right words to say, for she could hardly believe her ears. Suddenly the pain of misery started to recede from her brain. Her dream was coming true. Perhaps it was an expression of fear that the same thing might happen to them again as well as joy that Sidney was there to offer a helping hand. Alice sighed behind a soft smile and Stanley gave her a reassuring look.

"Well", dragging out the word for an extended moment, "if that is what you want, I think it would help us a lot," she replied with a lump in her throat and tears in her eyes so overwhelmed with joy was she. Stanley simply lit another cigarette and took three puffs with the kind of satisfaction that said it all. In those days there was no need for legal documentation or signed contract. It was an unwritten contract signed with a couple of drinks from a bottle of the finest Barbados rum. Alice slowly made her way back home with her meagre shopping wrapped in a small cloth. Within two hours the familiar blue smoke rising from the small galvanized kitchen into the branches of an overhanging mango tree indicated the evening meal was on its way. That evening after dinner as they sat during twilight reflecting on the day as they usually did, Alice drew on her spiritual background when she remarked, *God moves in mysterious ways.* She had always wished for a miracle: that someone would come along to ward off what could be another bout of distress. It was the fear of disaster striking for a ninth time.

It was about midnight six weeks later when Stanley lit the small kerosene lamp in the corner. The feeble gleam was enough for Elliot to see a measure of concern on his father's face when he woke him. "Go and fetch your grandmother quickly." Every pang of Alice's pain hit at the very pit of Stanley's stomach as he tried to comfort her for, although he had gone through this many times before, it did not reduce the ache he was experiencing. As he gazed into her eyes he could only see mixed feelings of expectation, apprehension, hope and despair imprinted on her face.

"Yes dad, I'll run as quickly as I can," replied Elliott setting out into the dark night with only the sound of whistling frogs and bush crickets to speed him on his way. Grand-mother grabbed her usual pair of scissors - the very one she had used many times before - and was soon at Alice's bedside. She was the village midwife who made use of the skills handed down through her Ashanti ancestry. It had just gone one in the morning when a shrill cry tore into the still night signalling the arrival of the latest member of the Atkins family. Waves of joy immediately filled the house. The fact that the baby was alive filled Alice with renewed hope and excitement. Grandmother tightened her head-tie before turning to Stanley.

"Get her a cup of hot milk and I would do with a coffee myself," she suggested. Sipping on her coffee quietly gave her time to notice that throughout such excitement, Alice was already battling with conflicting thoughts about the adoption. "I know what you are thinking Alice but do remember why we thought the idea of adoption was a good one. You have lactating problems so we thought that the adoption would give the little infant a better chance of survival," exclaimed grandmother who was herself the mother of thirteen children all of whom had lived into adult life. Alice thanked Stanley and managed a weary smile. "Yes mum, I know he is going and it hurts but I'll always be there for him," she replied before drifting into a sleep of sheer exhaustion all of which gave her mother a feeling of satisfaction.

Within two weeks of its birth, the new-born, dressed in a simple blue and white outfit, was handed over to Irene and Sidney its adopted parents in the presence of its grandmother. Alice was biting back a sob for it was heart-breaking going through such an experience, but they knew that the Redmans had the means to provide medical help and the kind of care and attention they themselves could not afford. Every time Alice heard the baby cry, it tugged at her heart. Part of her had gone with it. Yet they saw it as giving the baby a better chance of surviving. It was a win-win situation but it was the beginning of a journey that was to take that baby along a route strewn with some of the most bizarre and unforgettable experiences. The story is true, I know. I was that baby.

2

Off To School

*A*n October shower signalling the onset of the rainy season had brought momentary relief from the noon-day sun. Heat radiating from the foliage combined with the recent shower had produced a smell almost as pungent as that in the depth of an equatorial rain forest. A small flock of sparrows darted among nearby banana trees enjoying a bath and a drink from miniature pools of water trapped between the base of the leaves and trunk. A few cockerels and hens were in the back yard scratching away in the loose soil in search of succulent worms. The clang of old Sam's hoe could be heard in the distance as he turned the soil in preparation for planting in time for the coming rains. Sidney and Irene had not long finished lunch and were enjoying a cold drink of coconut water. Sidney placed his glass gently on the table and peered through the east window with a pensive look for a moment before slowly levelling his eyes with hers. She knew her husband well enough to know that such an expression after a silent pensive moment signalled he was about to say something significant. He took a deep audible breath. "I am going to buy that shop in Speightstown," he uttered. Irene nodded in quiet approval inclining her head regally. He had received word that a larger shop in Speightstown

9

was up for sale and they had already gone to see it.

Within three months from the 'hand-over' of baby Dennis, the Atkins made the move to Speightstown. Alice's eyes were filled with tears as she hugged me for the last time. "Please keep in touch," she whispered softly to my new parents, choking back the tears. I was taken from a small two gabled chattel house in a small rural village to a large stone building housing a shop and residential quarters in a town. It was here that I first became aware of the world around me: a world of tarmac roads, street lights, of electricity and tap water in the home, of shops and small stores, of people and traffic and of parents who loved me and did everything possible to make my childhood a happy one, ably assisted with the help of one other person of the household.

Lilian was a young woman of about twenty and the daughter of a poor white family who welcomed the opportunity of their daughter working for a middleclass family. She was short and wore her long dark hair in a pony-tail at the back but she was unfortunate not even to have a full elementary education without which, in spite of her colour, she stood little chance of getting one of the more privileged jobs in one of the large department stores or shops in Bridgetown or Speightstown even though It was a time when the colour of your skin determined the job you were likely to get. Lillian's lack of education was the product of her early ancestors who were 'indentured servants' from Scotland or Ireland during the reign of Oliver Cromwell. It was a community welcomed neither by the white society nor the black. As a result, it became isolated and suffered extreme poverty. Lilian's main job was to take care of me which she did admirably from a baby.

It was a large four-door shop in Speightstown, at that time the busiest port in Barbados. From here, ships laden with sugar, syrup and molasses left for Bristol and London after discharging their cargoes of timber, flour, salted cod, cooking oil and manufactured goods. First settled in 1630, this little seaside town was the settlement which Admiral Ayscue failed to take when dispatched by Oliver Cromwell of England to quell the insurrection in Barbados in 1649. The Redmans had made the right decision for, owning a large four-door shop in the nineteen forties and fifties, was like owning a small superstore in the nineties. Its location at the junction of Queen's Street, the main road between Speightstown and Bridgetown, and the road leading to the port meant it had a number of advantages. From here it attracted local trade, passing trade and that from the port especially when cargo vessels were in port. Unlike the previous shop, this was a stone building with the ground floor housing the shop, store room, kitchen and dining room and an upper floor housing the living quarters: bedrooms, sitting room, and a veranda that was opened on three sides and overlooked the road. The upper floor could also be reached by an exterior stone-stairs. Only the main road directly in front separated the shop from the golden sands of the west coast beach. The yard, in which there was one large cherry tree and two coconut trees, was fairly large and walled in. It was in this yard that I was to spend many a day playing with my friend from next door and where the shop attendants would sometimes play a game of cricket with invited friends.

* * * * * * * *

As the years rolled on, the next phase in my development arrived. About half-a-mile away at the junction of Chapel Street and Farm Road stood a small stone-built building - Speightstown Boys Elementary school. It was here that at the age of five I was launched into my school career. While in the veranda I would often see children on their way to and from school and I looked forward to joining them one day. It was something to which my parents also looked forward very much and they were no doubt anxious to see me begin the journey of formal education. From what they had seen like, for example, my ability to reproduce drawings of objects around me, they were confident I would do very well at school. But I can never forget that first day for it brought with it an experience that remained indelibly imprinted on my mind and, I am sure, on the minds of my parents.

I was on my back in bed gazing at the window through which the sun came peeping in at morn welcoming me to a new day. I could hear pigeons outside cooing in the cherry tree as they did almost every morning. It was part of a small flock which my dad kept to provide poultry as an alternative to meat on Sundays. But I could also hear Lillian's footsteps as she ascended the stairs to get me up. It was like any other morning with beams of sunlight entering my room intermittently broken by the shimmering movement of the cherry tree near the window. In another thirty minutes I was showered and made ready for school before having my breakfast.

My parents, who were already busy in the shop serving early customers, found time to pause for a while and admire their little boy dressed in his white shirt, short grey trousers and brown sandals and yes…a hanky in his pocket. They both kissed me and, with Lillian holding my hand firmly, we stepped out into the bright morning sunshine to begin my first journey. I looked back and there they were in the doorway hugging each other and smiling while waving me on. It was a wave which said, *"we will miss you darling but we hope you will be happy, my son."* Mum was fighting back tears as she looked at dad. "You think he'll be alright Sidney?" He turned slowly behind a warm, comforting look. "Oh, don't you worry my dear, our little boy will be fine." He adjusted his white apron and made his way to open a bag of rice. Colourfully dressed street vendors were already taking up their usual positions on the sidewalk at the front of the shop from where they served passing customers with fruit and vegetables and they would soon be joined by other vendors selling cold mauby (a beverage made from boiled buckthorn tree bark) to quench the thirst of those already suffering in the midmorning heat.

"But this will be the first time he will be away from us for so long Sidney and I am already beginning to miss him," she declared, a broken sob escaping from her lips as she wiped the tears from her eyes for, although she had no children of her own, she had very strong maternal feelings. She turned and slowly made her way back to serve a waiting customer who, seeing what was happening, placed her basket carefully on the counter and piped up, "don't worry Irene he'll be alright. They soon grow up. I know. I been through all of that with mine and it doesn't matter how many children you have, every time one has to start school, it is always a sad moment." Sidney and Irene were seeing their little boy move into a new phase of development. As for me, I was excited to know I was going to school like other children but I was also sad when I looked back and saw my parents waving me on. Everything looked strange that morning as Lillian and I made our way along Queen Street before turning into Chapel Street and pass the Methodist Church my mum attended and where I attended Sunday school. Dad was Anglican and took me to the parish church on Sunday nights.

On that first journey Lillian, seeing that I was getting a bit worried, gave me all the encouragement she could. She told me how I would make friends with other little boys with whom I would be playing in the school yard and how much I would like school and how nice I looked. As we drew nearer to the school I could hear children playing but I could also see other little boys like me with their mothers standing together inside the school gate or under the large tamarind tree in the school yard. With my hand firmly in Lilian's I stood there saying nothing. Fear of the unknown had gripped me. I was trembling on the inside for never before had I seen such a large gathering of boys, nor did the stern faces of teachers help as they went about preparing to start the new term. Lillian's comforting words fell on deaf ears. I knew no one and I felt no one knew me until I saw a familiar face coming through the school gate a few feet away.

"Hey Lillian look, there is Jack," I shouted, suddenly overflowing with excitement. Jack was one of the small boys with whom I was allowed to play on Saturdays. He would come to our house or I would be taken to his. Seeing Jack reduced some of my fear for I was now on more familiar ground with my friend. Like me, he was wearing short trousers held in place by a pair of straps, the kind that formed a large X across one's back. "Jack, Jack," I shouted, breaking into a broad smile. Jack quickly turned in my direction and, as if programmed, we both broke away and made for each other. It was nice to see someone I knew. Jack was a bit smaller than me and lived at a small two-door shop just around the corner not far from the school.

This short spell in our comfort zone was soon broken when the bell rang signalling the beginning of the school day and the start of our new journey. I said goodbye to Lillian who kissed me and Jack to his mother before making our way through the door. On entering the door, I looked up to see a burly figure looking down at me as I passed within inches of him. I was expecting a smile like that to which I was accustomed at home but his face remained motionless as though set in Plaster-of-Paris immediately sending shivers down my spine. It was not long before I discovered he was the head teacher. Nobody had told me what to expect but here I was in a small group of boys all standing quietly and wondering what happens next. I can hardly remember what we did in school that day so overcome with fear was I. In fact, I was so afraid all day that I could not even pluck up enough courage to ask the teacher's permission to go to the toilet. This resulted in me wetting my short grey trousers on my first day at school before morning break when we were given a cup of milk and two biscuits but the morning break gave me another chance to meet Jack and talk under the tamarind tree in the schoolyard. It was under this tree many weeks after that we were to join others in collecting the ripe tamarind pods that had fallen to the ground. After removing the outer shell, we would enjoy the thin, tasty flesh around each stone. Jack was as scared as me on that first day.

The large clock on the wall above the head teacher's desk struck twelve and the whole school stood up to recite a short prayer before lunch. Within minutes we were going through the school gate. I was looking anxiously for Lillian when suddenly there she was with a smile and outstretched arms to receive me. On seeing my mini-disaster the smile quickly evolved into a laugh, although with a degree of sympathy. "Oh dear, what have you done to yourself?" But, before I could say anything, she seemed to know why it had happened. I said nothing for I was so ashamed but I was soon home to a change of trousers and lunch. It never occurred again. Mum and dad also saw the funny side of it but showed much sympathy after I told them I was too afraid to go to the teacher, a fearsome looking character. They both comforted me with a hug and a kiss. Mum and dad would always come to the door to see me off with Lillian on mornings and after lunch. Like all the others in my class, I spent the next two years having the three Rs (reading, writing and arithmetic) drummed into me. It was the era of rote learning when reading was taught using the phonetic method and when the times tables were drilled into you; teacher would often hold my hand and help me to form letters on my slate. I enjoyed the nursery rhymes and could often be heard reciting them while playing at home. I grew to like school very much.

3

Sundays At The Redmans'

*L*iving by the sea brought its pleasures but none more so than when dad took me with him to the beach on Sunday mornings. It was usually about nine o'clock when he would say, *"Come little fellow, we are going to the beach."* My eyes would sparkle as I ran around telling everyone I was going to the beach with dad. With towels safely tucked under our arms we would cross the main road and enter a short footpath taking us through a small coconut grove. Most of the trees always seemed to be laden with bunches of coconuts, some green but others brown and dry having remained on the tree too long. Some were even bent so low toward the sea that they seemed to be greeting the shallow incoming waves making their way up the beach. Small boys would often be seen spending much time trying to see how far they could walk along the almost horizontal trunk before falling on the soft sand. Others would be splashing around in the shallow water or making shapes in the sand. By then the sun would be high enough in the sky to make its presence felt with beams that sparkled softly on the azure blue west coast Caribbean waters.

In less than ten minutes we would be emerging from the grove and stepping onto a wide expanse of golden sand caressed by gentle waves creeping up the shore and, after depositing their load of small sea shells and baby crabs, showing reluctance to return as little ripples to the sea. Here where the west coast beach nudges the tranquil waters of the Caribbean Sea in all its turquoise glory, was my stretch of paradise. These almost white sands, blue skies and calm west coast waters provided an environment to which I eagerly looked forward on Sunday mornings. My dad, who was a very good swimmer, would put me on his back and ask me to put my hands around his neck. *"Now you hold on tight,"* he would say, so there I would be, perched on his back as he swam along the shore. Around us I could see through the clear crystal water shoals of small fish - grey, blue, silver and multi-coloured - darting here and there in an underwater display of colour that glistened under the rays of the tropical sun. "Can you see the fish?" he would often ask, the water flowing off his light brown back with every rise and fall as he glided smoothly on his breaststroke.

"Yes dad, they are pretty…but will they grow big?" I would say, my face getting bathed every now and then as my dad simply glided smoothly through the water. My eyes seemed to capture every harmonious twist and turn of these submarine gymnasts. At times I felt like putting my hand out and touching this living patchwork of colour - an underwater wonder world - as they swam along with us but dad always told me to hold on tightly

"Oh yes… most of them will and you may even eat some of them one day," he would say with a chuckle while I hung on in wonderment. After the swim, we would spend some time together making pools in the sand. If any of my friends were around, I would be allowed to play in the sand with them while dad would be lying flat on his back or just sitting and looking out to sea, or maybe having a chat and a laugh with my friends'

Walking Through The Pain

parents for most locals made a point of going to the sea on Sunday mornings. Soon it was time to have a final dip in the water to get rid of any excess sand and a quick rub down before making our way back home through the grove. It was always an enjoyable morning.

Attending church on Sundays was an integral part of family life in Barbados. It provided an occasion to display some of your best clothes. Men were usually well turned out in their immaculate white or grey suits and well-polished brown or black shoes while women added to the scene in their colourful frocks, stylish hats and handbags. After a week of toil and labour, it provided an opportunity for churchgoers to sing to their hearts content and, probably, to rid themselves of some of the frustrations of the week. But it was also a social occasion when, after service, folk gathered together in small groups to meet friends and discuss the happenings of the week.

After a shower to remove any residue of sand, I would be dressed and ready to accompany my mum to the small Methodist church for 11 o'clock service. To me, it was always very hot by that time which, when combined with an hour or so at the sea and the walk to church, would leave me drained to the point where I would soon be asleep on a bench to the whispering sound of a light cooling breeze stealing its way through an open window. I would only come alive again on hearing the gentle voice of my mum calling, *"Dennis, come son, it's time to go home now."* These words always came floating on a motherly smile as she gently lifted me from the bench and got me ready to go. After giving my eyes a quick rub I would soon be on my way with my hand safely in hers. At times she would stop to have a quick chat with a friend or two also on their way home from church. This I didn't like very much. *"Why does she have to stop and speak with people? I just want to get home out of the hot sun*

19

and get a drink." All I could think of is what we were having for Sunday lunch so I was in no mood to wait around while mum chatted. It was difficult to be polite and not make it known to mum that I wanted to go although I am sure she usually got the message from my growing but quiet uneasiness. I knew the conversation would be coming to an end when I heard, *"I must go now because this little fellow is getting restless and I know he may be getting a bit hungry."* Such words were always music to my ears.

Sunday lunch was always a special occasion. Sometimes aunt Daisy, my dad's sister, would spend a few days with us during the school holidays. I always looked forward to her visits because she took me for walks in the town centre and she always played games with me. But she would also teach me how to read and write using some of the books she brought with her, for she was a teacher. Together, we also spent much time in the veranda from where she would explain what was going on below as well as in the port. Although I did not understand most of the jokes shared at the table, the fact that we were all together sitting at the table enjoying lunch and the laughter that accompanied it, told me that Sunday lunch was a special occasion.

With lunch over, my dad would then entertain us with his small collection of vinyl tunes on the gramophone: a collection of hymns and popular songs of the day. It usually turned out that he would soon be fast asleep in his rocking chair near the window, leaving the music to be seen to by mum or Lillian or even aunt Daisy. Sundays brought a kind of stillness: coopers' hammers in the nearby cooperage were dormant; no horse-drawn carts or trucks going to and from the port normally alive with the hustle and bustle creating that familiar din; shops remained closed and, apart from the snow-ball cart, there were no street vendors to be seen; even buses were less frequent. It was a time too when most people remained indoors except for those going to church or to the beach. It was a time when Sundays in Barbados were kept hallowed: no work for adults and no playing outside for children. It was treated as a day of rest.

Sunday school was not an occasion I liked very much. I saw it as cutting into the quality time I spent with my mum and dad. Lillian would often take me along what she called a shortcut - through Mango Lane. In fact, it was the same back lane along which she would sometimes take me to day school. Here the land was so flat that you would come across the occasional small pool of stagnant water which attracted swarms of dragonflies their bodies reflecting a hovering display of rainbow colours in the bright afternoon sun. On the way I would pass some of my friends' houses, a collection of gabbled and four-hipped chattel houses and each displaying its own colour but usually with a Croton at the front displaying its ornamental foliage. A group of small boys would often be playing marbles in the sand or some other game instead of being dressed up in a sailor suit and going to Sunday school.

"Lillian, can I play with those boys a little bit?" would often be my request, willing her to say yes.

"No Dennis, you are not allowed to play out on Sundays especially when you are going to Sunday school," would be her firm reply. Instead, we would continue along the lane passing tall grass reaching almost up to my head and pea-trees with branches sometimes so heavy with peas that they straddled the ditch and hung over the path. I often wondered why I could not be like some of those boys who played in the sand on Sunday afternoons. Perhaps mum and dad were telling me something I couldn't understand at that time. On my return from Sunday school, my dad would take me for a Sunday evening walk on the jetty but it was on one such walk that I lost something very dear to me, my sailor hat. We had almost reached the end of the jetty when a sudden gust of wind snatched my hat and deposited it out to sea.

"Dad, dad, my hat", I screamed, looking up and willing him to do something. He was focused on a large ship far out to sea but, on hearing my scream, he jerked his head in haste in my direction just in time to see my hat settling gently on the waves. He was a good swimmer but he was not prepared to remove his Sunday evening suit and go after a hat. He held my hand tightly and bent forward levelling his eyes with mine. "Never mind Dennis, don't cry, I'll buy you another one soon." This promise, supported with a candy from his pocket, did the job.

We sat on a bench for a while watching the tropical sunset. The sinking sun was casting its golden horizontal rays on an almost calm sea while throwing a glow on a residue of clouds above against a sky that was now fast turning a lighter shade of purple. Against this backdrop, we were entertained by a shoal of flying fish leaping into the air seemingly in concert with the sound of small waves lapping gently against the posts that supported the jetty. As I watched my sailor hat carried further and further out to sea with every passing breeze, many thoughts and images invaded my mind. *"I wonder if someone will find it or will I ever see it again? Perhaps one day it might be washed ashore somewhere."* Such was the imagination of a little boy of six. I returned home that evening with a sailor suit minus a sailor hat. Many times as I stood in the veranda looking out onto the jetty I often thought of my hat making its way to some distant land.

But Sunday was not always about going to church or going for a stroll on the jetty. Occasionally we would have a visit from family friends in Boscobel, a village near the east coast. The

Walking Through The Pain

Carringtons also owned a shop in this more rural part of St Peter which meant they had a lot in common to talk about with my parents. They would usually arrive for afternoon tea, a British characteristic introduced no doubt by those early planters from the United Kingdom. It was an occasion for their daughter Celeste and me to enjoy generous helpings of cake and homemade ice-cream served in pink sundae glasses against a background of music from my dad's gramophone. Celeste was about my age and always wore pink ribbons in her hair. Together we would spend much time reading picture books or just sitting in the veranda looking out to sea or chatting for, like our parents, we too had a lot in common to chat about. I always looked forward to our return visits to the Carringtons.

During the week as I sat in the veranda looking out to the jetty I could see four-wheeled wagons loaded with bags of sugar or barrels of syrup and molasses, each trundled by two men along a set of rails. From there, they would be loaded onto small boats and taken out to the much larger ocean-going cargo vessels. The little port had no deep water facilities hence the use of smaller boats, 'lighters' they were called, for transferring commodities to and from the jetty. Crop time was certainly the busiest time of the year when trucks would be descending on the port but it was the daily rhythmic sound of hammers as coopers went about the business of fixing metal bands around barrels that fascinated me most. To me it seemed as though each hammer had its own unique musical sound although it was the combined sound and rhythm that gave me a thrill.

4

Who Are These People?

The veranda became my favourite place in the house although I was not allowed to go there unless supervised in case I did something silly like try to climb over and end up in a mess on the street below. Buses passing below were so close that I sometimes felt like putting my hand out and touching the tops. From this vantage point I would also observe the ice-cream man or even the snowball man selling crushed ice to which he added a colouring of red or yellow syrup. He was always hemmed in by small boys jostling with each other to be served. It all added to my excitement on many a day but it was the jetty, less than two hundred yards away, that was to bring me face to face with another side of reality.

School holidays had arrived allowing me more time to spend in my favourite observation spot. From my ringside seat, I could see a large cargo vessel at anchor discharging its cargo. It was from here too that I would make pencil drawings of the ship with its funnels pumping out columns of black smoke and cranes lowering large items into small boats. I could tell it was a very busy day in the port from the many trucks making their way to and from the wharf. Horse-drawn carts loaded with lumber from

25

the nearby lumber yard were leaving for outlying villages. I was enjoying a mid-afternoon drink of cold lemonade and a piece of cake when the dragging of chairs and the sweeping sound of a broom told me that Lillian was not far away. She was cleaning the sitting room while keeping a sharp eye on me. Leaving the veranda, I headed for that piece of furniture I always cherished - the rocking chair. From here I would watch her glide between the mahogany cane-bottom chairs as I rocked gently. We were talking about school and the friends I made when suddenly my attention was shattered by the wailing sound of a vehicle speeding over to the jetty. Never before had I heard such a sound or seen such a vehicle. With eyes popping and pieces of cake shooting from my mouth I darted back to the veranda with such speed that, had the veranda not been enclosed, I would have ended up on the street below.

"What's that Lillian?" I shouted, expecting an answer as hastily as I had dispatched the question. She looked as curious as me for, although she obviously knew what it was, she was anxious to know why it was speeding towards the jetty. With a duster in one hand she held me tightly with the other. We were now both focusing on the jetty where the mid-afternoon sun was beating down mercilessly on animate and inanimate objects alike. Hammers in the cooperage suddenly fell silent. Carts trundling along the rails on the jetty came to a halt. A steady stream of onlookers took up position near the jetty, expressions on their faces indicating the hurt they felt as men, hardly able to walk, were hauled up a short gangway from small boats and hurried off to waiting ambulances. The atmosphere was impregnated with the smell of oil and burnt flesh. It was my first experience of what war meant. It was during the Second World War.

"That's an ambulance," replied Lillian, fixing her eyes on the growing number of people making their way to the jetty. It was a crowd swollen by workers from the lumber yard, the cooperage and passers-by. Even the bus on its way to Bridgetown stopped for a moment to allow passengers to see what was going on and, as usual, it provided a perfect opportunity for the more knowledgeable to voice their understanding of what was happening. A cargo vessel had been bombed and sunk at sea within Caribbean waters and the survivors were from that burning ship. Many days after, the west coast beaches were littered with large tins of corned beef, barrels of salted cod, bags of flour, boxes of partly singed clothing and much more for which there was no shortage of takers with bags, baskets and boxes to gather what they could from the washed up items.

"Ambulance, what's an ambulance?" I snapped, standing on tiptoe with my chin resting on the rail to get a good view, "and why all these people?" I added while looking at her with my face tightly squeezed in anticipation of quick answers.

"It takes sick people to hospital, Dennis," she said with a long drawn-out groan as though she too was suffering pain. She had come to learn a bit of what war meant from the daily BBC news on the radio from London but never before had she witnessed such a scene.

"But who is sick out there? Nobody lives on the jetty Lillian." Before she could respond the quick build-up of the crowd told me something quite unusual was happening. My curiosity was soon satisfied for, emerging in the distance, were men helped to walk by others. With clothes torn to shreds and bodies completely drenched in black oil, I could smell the stench even from our veranda. The only thing that told me they were people was the white of their eyes and teeth as they grimaced with pain. Amidst the sounds of still more speeding ambulances and everybody shouting instructions, they were helped aboard to be raced to the hospital in Bridgetown about eleven miles away. Some, who were not too badly hurt, were hurriedly brought to our place to be cleaned up before making the journey. The back room was suddenly a busy place with people coming and going and the shower at the far end going non-stop with the pungent smell of carbolic soap filling the air.

This was all too much for me. I broke away from Lillian and raced across the floor tripping over a broom she had left in the way and ending up in the rocking chair in the corner next to the gramophone. Pulling myself together quickly, I scampered down the stairs head down and with such speed that I failed to see my dad standing at the foot. It was as though he was expecting me for, before I could come to a halt, my head had slammed firmly against his belly.

"What's the matter, son? Why are you running down the stairs like that?"

"Dad," I croaked, "who are these people? Where are they from? Why do they look so dirty?" My screwed-up face suggested I wanted quick answers. I am not sure whether it was fear, curiosity or excitement as I looked up at him with a kind of rigid determination that made it somewhat difficult for words to leave my mouth. He drew me closer to him and looked into my eyes and I could see he was trying to find a way of explaining the whole experience to me.

"They are survivors," he said with a concerned look.

"Survivors dad!" I asked hastily, "who are survivors dad?" my face resembling a stewed prune for I was already thoroughly confused with ambulances, police vans, sirens, men in rags covered in black oil and now survivors. Customers in the shop had also positioned themselves to witness the drama and, like those standing near the jetty, were also quick to demonstrate their understanding of what was going on in a vociferous manner. Put all of this together and you might have a close-up of what I was experiencing that mid-afternoon. My dad held me close to him again. It was as though he could see that, young as I was, I too felt the pain and discomfort these men were suffering.

"Survivors are seamen who manage to survive a burning ship after it has been bombed" said dad, no doubt hoping that it would be enough to quell my curiosity which he was finding somewhat difficult to do.

"Bombed, what do you mean by bombed dad, I don't see any fire and smoke?" I snapped finding it somewhat difficult to put meaning to what he was saying although I managed to associate smoke and fire with bombs. Perhaps I had picked it up from comments made on evenings by the usual group gathered around the radio to hear what was happening at the front during the war.

"No Dennis, the ship was bombed and sunk far out to sea. They escaped in small boats and paddled their way to the jetty." I looked at him with gaping mouth for it was taking some time for me to wrap my little brain around what he was saying.

"But the people who did that to them are wicked, aren't they dad?"

"Yes son," he replied with the usual gentle tap on my head.

"I hope they don't come and bomb our house and who are those two women dressed like that and wearing those funny white hats?" "They are called nurses and they are helping to clean up

Dean Alleyne

the survivors. You remember when you cut your toe on an empty sardine tin and I took you to a building just up the road to get it attended to?"

"Yes dad, I remember. You took me on your back with my toe tied up."

"Well, they are some of the same nurses you can see there." Sidney looked around to see a line of survivors being helped to the back room. "Bob, Gordon, see to the customers, I want to give a helping hand in the back." Bob and Gordon were long-standing shop attendants. As I ambled my way up the stairs to re-join Lillian, I kept wondering if those survivors had seen my sailor hat out at sea. This, my first glimpse of what war meant, was supported by frequent 'blackouts' at night. The shop would usually be busy when suddenly all lights including street lights would go out accompanied by the wailing sound of a siren. My dad often did his best to explain this to me.

Our shop was the first port-of-call for arriving seamen. Here they mingled and chatted with the locals over a rum or beer or other ice-cold drinks like mauby, a very popular drink in parts of the Caribbean. Failing that, it would be lemonade, ginger beer, or coconut water. This would usually be accompanied with a salt beef, ham, or cheese cutter, or even a fried fish cutter. A cutter was a large loaf cut halfway through and filled with any one of the above: very delicious when garnished with a touch of home-made hot pepper sauce. The very smell of freshly cooked salt beef or ham from the bone was enough to whet the appetite of anyone. All this took place in the bar in one corner of the shop. It was a bar you entered through a revolving door like something out of a western movie, except that I can't ever recall anyone being thrown head first through it into the street.

Walking Through The Pain

Shops were not allowed to be opened on Sundays but, in order not to lose trade whenever a cargo vessel was in port, my parents would offer a restaurant service upstairs reached by external stone stairs. It was here that, against a background of vinyl tunes on the gramophone, seamen enjoyed a nice home-cooked meal and caught up with the latest happenings on the island. Such customers would often show their appreciation with gifts from foreign lands: small radios, watches, perfumes or even gold rings. For me, it was usually wound-up toys not yet seen on the island. On one occasion I was even given a very small gold ring supposedly from Guyana (then British Guyana) from where the ship had sailed and where gold was mined. I was too small to appreciate its value so I hid it under my pillow that evening for safe keeping, or so I thought. It was the kind of thing a small boy of seven would do. I awoke next morning to find it had gone but it didn't matter too much to me for at my age, I was more interested in toys than a gold ring.

The bar did very well especially on Saturday nights or when there was world heavyweight boxing, an event that attracted people from all around to listen to the blow-by-blow commentary from one of the few radios in Speightstown. For any radio to function in the 1940s it had to have an aerial which was a special piece of wire extended for a number of meters and suspended on a pole outside. You would disturb this wire at your peril for to do so even by chance would mean an abrupt end to transmission followed by an outburst of verbal violence on the offending culprit sometimes ending in physical combat. The air was always filled with continuous comments from those who boasted some knowledge of boxing. Sometimes it was a skirmish, verbal or otherwise, only brought to an abrupt halt when someone shouted *Shussssh...shut yah big mout and leh me hear what's going on*. Very often this suggested that something

31

dramatic had happened, like a 'knockout' bringing the whole stadium in Madison Square Garden or wherever to its feet and often accompanied by a tumultuous applause so deafening as to make it impossible to hear any further commentary.

Nor was it unusual for up to twenty men to descend upon the shop on evenings to await the chimes of Big Ben followed by the words, *this is London calling in the world service of the BBC.* It signalled the entry of a newsreader or Winston Churchill himself to give an update on what was happening at the war front. It was the kind of news eagerly awaited by all each one keen to voice their opinion on the situation. I would occasionally be awakened by the tumultuous uproar from the group when a heavy blow was dealt on German forces and it was a time when the name Winston Churchill was on everyone's lips.

5

A Mother's Love

As the years rolled on, my biological parents, brothers, grandparents, aunts and uncles came to see me as often as possible, most visits taking place on weekends. I can remember the first time I was conscious of a visit from my biological mother and it was the first time I got to know her. That Saturday the shop was heaving with customers rushing mum, dad and the attendants off their feet. Frequent trips were made to the sugar, rice or flour bags from which full scoops would be taken and placed on scales with copper made scale-pans. There was an almost unbroken series of thuds from the two scales as attendants tried to strike a balance. Such a scale was the kind of contraption that depended a lot on judgment but that made a bang every time the heavier side hit the base. Others would be chopping chunks of salt pork or salt beef or parcelling red-herring, the smell of which permeated every nook and cranny of the shop, while someone would be serving in the bar.

The coopers' hammers were hard at work when I heard *mauby cool, come and get it.* It was a street vendor with a large container of cold mauby on her head making her way to the port. It seemed to whet my appetite for I was soon busy gathering ripe juicy cherries that had fallen from the tree just outside my bedroom window. But it was the busy hubbub in the shop that morning that attracted my attention most. I was not allowed to go into the shop but, sitting on a bench from a suitable vantage point, I could observe the hustle and bustle while stuffing myself with the red fruit from which juice trickled down both sides of my bulging mouth as I popped them in and ejected small stones from my lips like miniature bullets. My mum would often use these cherries to make a very tasty jam which I liked very much and which she would share with friends and neighbours.

The busy hubbub and the din from the many conversations among customers did not prevent me from noticing a woman entering through the far door. She was short and wore a very light brown hat that almost blended with her skin. I could tell she was not from Speightstown because, unlike the other women entering the shop, she carried on her head a basket full of things which I later learned were breadfruit, sweet potatoes, pumpkin, green peas, a little bit of everything grown in her plots of land. She lowered the basket from her head and, with sweat trickling down her face, looked at me with a warm smile that told me she was different. Dad was pouring a measure of cooking oil into a customer's bottle when the heavy thud of the basket on the counter caused him to jerk his head quickly around. "Oh, hello Alice," he said with the broadest of smiles and with excitement rising to the point where he was unaware that the oil was overflowing. This moment, fleeting though it was, caught the attention of other customers who looked around to see what was causing this sudden upsurge in excitement. Before Alice could respond, mum came from the bar where she was serving drinks to two men who worked on the jetty but who obviously felt in need of some mid-morning liquid refreshments.

"Nice to see you again Alice, give me the basket. You come

around," she uttered. Soon Alice was in the back room sitting where she could take advantage of every passing breeze. This little woman kept smiling at me as though she was anxious to say something but was waiting for the right moment. I was now standing in the doorway when mum gazed at her and then at me and with an affectionate smile said, "Come here Dennis." I moved slowly toward her while keeping my eyes fixed on this little woman who was given special treatment. "Say hello to your mother." I glared at her. It was the word *mother* that totally confused me. She didn't have to ask me twice for before the words could leave her mouth my mother was wrapping me in her arms and smothering me with kisses. I looked at her curiously but lovingly, confused though I was. Sitting on her knee and with my hand on her left shoulder, I gazed firmly into her greenish-brown eyes. Just then a cool breeze wafting its way through a nearby window seemed to engulf us with a feeling of quiet belonging.

"Where do you live?" I asked with an inquiring look similar to the one used when I was inquiring about ambulances and survivors. She looked at me with a soft smile.

"I live in a little village far away from here called St Simons and it is so far that I had to set out very early this morning and walk all the way before it got too hot." Small though I was, I could see from her exhausted look that she had a tiresome journey.

"Are there no buses?" I asked, because I couldn't understand why she had to walk all the way for, apart from going to school or church, I had been everywhere by bus.

"No, there are no buses that run from St Simons to Speightstown." Her voice trailed off as she cast an understanding look at me.

"You walked from so far with that heavy basket on your head?" I

Dean Alleyne

was now feeling and looking very distressed that she had to do such a journey carrying such a load on her head in the hot sun.

"Yes my son." As she said this, wiping the sweat from her brow, I could feel something drawing me closer to her. It was an inner feeling which, though light as air, was as strong as an iron band. She told me about my father whom I often saw, brothers and the remainder of the family living back in St Simons, assuring me that I would see them one day. It was the kind of conversation a loving mother would carry on with her six-year old son. She told me about the wide open pastures, the cows, the sheep and goats, the rivers and hills and the fruit trees and much more. She could see I was excited as she spoke for my eyes popped with sheer imagination. Dad left the attendants in charge and joined us for a quick lunch and we had a wonderful time together but, as there was no cross-country bus between St. Simons and Speightstown, my mother would have to walk the long distance back home which meant she had to leave in a reasonable time in order not to be caught in the dark on the return journey. It was one that would take her through small villages up and down hills and along winding paths between fields of sugar cane. Soon, with her basket packed with tins of corned beef, salmon, sardines, small packets of flour, sugar and other items, goodbyes were exchanged between mother, mum and dad. After smothering me with yet more kisses, she safely placed the basket on her head and with that maternal smile, turned and started the three-hour return journey home on foot.

Although it was the first time I had seen my biological mother, her tender touch and motherly attention brought a kind of sadness over me as I watched her disappear slowly in the distance. With my imagination fired up I drew closely to my mum as we waved. "Mum, you mean I have two mums and two dads?" I looked to her to help me understand what was happening. Without going

36

Walking Through The Pain

into too much detail, she tried to explain what took place. I can't say I understood but what I do know is that I always saw my adopted parents as my 'first parents'. These were the parents with whom I first became conscious of the world around me although I also grew to know and love my biological parents very much. Often, as I lay quietly in my bed at night, I would think of my mother carrying that basket all the way and of the hills and valleys and open pastures far away about which she told me.

During the months and years that followed I had regular visits from my father and Elliot. My father always used a peddle-bike for the journey. I could tell my dad and my father enjoyed themselves by the laughter brought about from the many jokes they shared over a bottle of rum and coconut water. It seemed as though they were carrying on from where they had left off in St. Simon's. In some ways I became closer to my biological father than my biological mother in those early years, perhaps it was because I saw him more often. My mother no doubt was too occupied at home which meant she had very few days available for visiting. Just occasionally I would be in time to see my father approaching in the distance with a bag slung over the handle of his bike or strapped to a carrier at the back. I always knew what was in that bag: mangoes, cashews, golden apples and even pieces of soft sugar cane as well as home-made bread and cake, all from my mother. I would soon be in the yard slowly ploughing through a fruit or piece of home-made bread or even sharing it with a friend who had come over to play. In the yard were two tall coconut trees which swayed gently in the breeze but it was the cherry tree which reached up to my bedroom window that offered me and my friend shade from the mid-afternoon sun as we sat chatting and laughing about things small boys found amusing while stuffing their faces.

Of my two older brothers, Elliott was the one who visited me

37

most frequently. He was still at school but often spent most of his holidays with us in Speightstown. He helped in the shop and did daily chores but he also found time to spend with me either playing a ball game or going for short walks along Mango Lane less than two hundred yards away where he would also find friends to have a chat and a laugh. Sometimes he took me to the beach although I was not allowed to go swimming on his back like I did with dad. At other times we would just sit in the tall grass in the nearby open field and listen to the wind rustling through the grass while enjoying a piece of salted codfish and raw onion with biscuits. It was always good fun having him around especially at Christmas. I got very close to Elliot and grew to love him. Calvin hardly ever visited and so I don't think we ever got to know each other well.

Christmas was special for me like for many children. Lillian would help me hang my Christmas stocking at my bed head which in itself brought great excitement and anticipation at the thoughts of what Santa could be bringing me. I would awake on Christmas morning to find it full of wonderful gifts which I could hardly wait to remove from their coloured wrappings so excited would I be. It was a feeling magnified by the glow of the many coloured lights on the Christmas tree and the smell of fresh coffee wafting up the stairs. Soon and still in my pyjamas I would be joined by dad, mum, Lillian and Elliot, if he was spending Christmas with us, to open gifts under the tree around which we would dance. After our Christmas morning breakfast, I would spend most of the day playing with my wind-up toys or looking through my new picture books against a background of carols from the gramophone. It was always a very happy day for me.

During the crop season a lorry would sometimes pull up in front of the shop. Stepping down and making his way into the shop would be a tall, light skinned man with straight hair, carrying a small bundle of sugar cane. It was my uncle Dillon who was a driver at the sugar factory some distance away and was one of those taking bags of sugar to the nearby wharf. He visited very often during crop time eventually becoming my favourite uncle for I always looked to him for my sugar cane and sometimes boiled cane juice from the factory. I also grew very close to one of my aunts, Ersil who also came to see me very often when she was on holiday from Curacao. It was the sheer delight of seeing them that made them my favourites for, included in their sacks, were always things they knew I liked very much.

But, topping the list of all my visitors, was my biological maternal grand-dad, well-built and of Scottish ancestry, perhaps the fourth or fifth generation of one of those Scots who had migrated to Barbados in its early colonial days. He would arrive either on horseback or in a horse-drawn trap (a little buggy), the kind often seen in films based on life in the southern states of America. He made a point of seeing me at least once every month. As soon as he stepped down from his horse or buggy, he would take out his silver pocket watch and check the time. Like any other small boy, I was always fascinated by the watch chain dangling on the waistcoat of his white suit. He was not the kind of man to indulge in hugging and kissing but this didn't mean he loved me less than any other member of the family for he always made sure he spent maximum time with me whenever he visited. We would usually be seen sitting together on a bench in the yard under the cherry tree: the very tree that interrupted the flow of sunshine penetrating my window and flooding my bedroom on mornings.

He would tell me many things about the kind of life he had while working as a foreman in the goldfields of Guyana. He would tell me of times when he and his gang of workers would return some evenings to the camp to find someone's hammock swaying gently even though there was hardly a wind. The unwelcomed

Dean Alleyne

occupant was often a coiled-up snake which he would dispatch with one slash of his cutlass. Or of a worker who, in his search for a quiet place to sit and have his lunch, would sit on what appeared to be a tree stump covered with dead leaves until the warmth of his body would trigger a slight movement from the snake causing him to spring into the air like a bullet from a gun.

"But were you afraid of all those snakes and crocodiles, grand-dad?"

"No son, but you had to be very careful at all times."

"What else did you see there, grand-dad?"

"Oh, there are many birds of all colours: birds like the umbrella bird, the bellbird, colourful parrots and flamingos and in the swamps near the river you would see the Orinoco crocodile. Sometimes you would see crocodiles on the river bank basking in the sunshine or even skinless floating down river." I had never heard of or seen any of those birds or animals before and yet, even though such stories often sent shivers down my spine, I wanted to know more.

"And what about the people who lived there. Did they have electricity and roads and buses and houses like ours and shops?" On this occasion we were each enjoying a jam-puff and a drink while sitting in our usual place under the cherry tree. He wasn't too sure I would be able to take the stories he was telling me about his life in the gold mines of Demerara but since I didn't show any visible signs of dislike he thought he could tell me more. He dabbed his face to remove some beads of sweat trickling into his eyes before continuing.

"Where I was, there were no roads like those we have here.

40

Roads in that part were mainly gravel and dirt, not smooth like ours and because it rains so often, they are usually muddy. Most people live near the river in houses built on stilts over the water and tend to move around in small boats or canoes." His conversations would often be finished with *"Son, you will not understand everything I am telling you now, but one day when you grow up, I am sure you will,"* with the usual broad smile creeping across his freckled face thought to be brought about by the skin trying to adapt to the intensive heat of a tropical sun.

Although I never understood much of what he said, I always nodded in approval for, even at that tender age, I was always glad to be with him and to listen to what he had to say. Another frequently used statement of his was, *"you must try to do well at school because I would like you to have a profession."* He would often say this in the presence of my dad and mum adding, *"this little fellow must have the best education we can afford."* My dad and mum had no problem supporting this having noticed I had a flair for art as shown by the many drawings I often did of boats and things to do with the sea even at that tender age. What else could they be? After all, boats and the sea made up part of my physical environment. I would often run up to dad or mum holding a piece of paper with a drawing, "dad, look at my boat." He would look at it with great delight and say, "that's very good." This also pleased my grand-dad whose face would often turn bright red particularly if he had a few drinks with my dad.

6

Double Disaster

The shop was doing well and dad had taken mum and me to see a car he wanted to buy: a convertible, the kind suited to tropical conditions. Most of his friends who owned shops had cars and so he thought it the suitable thing to do and he had already test-driven it. Mum was looking forward to learning to drive in order to visit friends and family in various corners of the island more difficult to reach by bus. It was something we were all excited about. I was making new friends at school and life was beautiful for me, a little boy. But this was soon to be brought to an abrupt and unexpected end, one that was to change our lives forever. Aunt Daisy was on one of her usual holiday visits when, after dinner, she looked at dad with some concern. She was very observant and perceptive and was very good at seeing through her brother. She had noticed a change in his mood when she last visited two months before and again on the current visit but she was reluctant to mention it in the presence of Irene who had just then left the table for a few minutes to prepare an after-dinner drink.

"Are you feeling okay Sidney because you don't look too well." Her eyes were filled with concern beneath a frowned forehead.

43

Dean Alleyne

He didn't appear to her to be as lively and jovial and she was convinced something was worrying him. He didn't seem to be his usual self on this visit. Even when a joke was made at the dinner table he merely responded with a grin. Lillian had also noticed this and had quietly brought it to the attention of Irene who had suggested on a number of occasions that he ought to see the doctor but he never found the time to do so. But, seeing the concern on his sister's face, he drew his chair nearer to hers.

"I'm feeling alright except that I keep getting this pain in my side sometimes," he whispered not wanting mum to hear but it was too late. She had heard my aunt's comment and immediately interjected. "I keep telling him to go to the doctor and have it checked out but he keeps putting it off," she shouted from the kitchen, much to dad's surprise. "Okay, I'll go to the doctor tomorrow," he promised. It turned out to be a rumbling appendix which now had to be removed without delay.

On the morning he was leaving for the hospital we were all up earlier than usual as he was taking the seven o'clock bus to Bridgetown. I was still in my pyjamas when I came downstairs in time to see him take a lime, cut it into two pieces and squeeze all the juice of one piece into his mouth. He appeared to have a slight cough hence the lime juice. That morning he did not sweep the pavement in front of the shop as he always did, dressed in his white apron. Instead, he left that to one of the attendants. There to see him off were mum, Lillian and I. He placed his felt fedora hat on his head, kissed us all and said to me as I looked up at him from beside the table, "Now little Dennis, you be a nice boy until I get back." I nodded but, as he said that, I had a sinking feeling. I didn't quite know what was going on but tossing around in my little mind were thoughts like: *Would I ever see him again? Will he be back? Why can't I go with him?*

At that point, the bread van drew up as usual in front of the shop to deliver freshly baked bread. A couple of customers had already popped in to get their supply on way to work. The nearby coopers were already striking up that chorus of hammer against metal and lighter-men were also trundling tram carts on the rails carrying bags of sugar or barrels of syrup bound for a cargo vessel anchored beyond the jetty. Dad gave mum another kiss before taking his small suitcase to make his way to the bus waiting in front of the shop. We had been accustomed to seeing him take the bus every other week for Bridgetown to place his grocery order but this time it seemed different. He sat at the back and we watched him waving as the red bus disappeared slowly in the distance and, as I turned, I again wondered if he would ever come back. Mum was fighting back tears while waving at the disappearing bus for quite some time, the wave becoming smaller and smaller. There she stood for some time saying nothing only gazing into the distance. She held my hand. "Come Dennis," she said in a soft trembling voice as we walked slowly back indoors.

Mum went to see him the next day and on her return she was faced with "how is he doing?" from shop attendants and customers alike. I looked up at her with anxious eyes, "mum, how is dad, when is he coming back?" She shook her head, unable to speak for a moment. Lillian brought her a glass of water but her eyes looked glazed and her hand was shaking as she held the glass. On the following day mum took me with her to see dad. She held me closely to her as we sat in the bus on our way to Bridgetown. Nothing much was said but, small as I was, I sensed things had not gone the way she expected. Going through the large iron gates of the hospital I was immediately hit by the strong smell of disinfectant driving an all-enveloping fear throughout my body. Mum held my hand tightly as we entered one door and then another to reach the ward.

Neither of us was ready for what we were to see. It was a scene for which I was not prepared. There was dad lying on a bed and covered up to his shoulders with a white sheet. In a small cupboard next to him were his clothes, shoes and felt fedora. Nurses, dressed similar to those I had seen that day when the survivors came ashore, moved gracefully between his and other beds. Mum stood by his bedside for a long silent moment. Tears welling up in her heavy eyes eventually overflowed. I stood quietly at the foot of the bed watching my dad toss his head from side to side but saying nothing. He knew neither of us. I knew because he didn't respond when mum called his name. There was no way mum could have prepared me for this. We spent about an hour with dad before making our way back through the wrought-iron gates. I looked up at her face her eyes now red with tears.

"Mum, what's wrong with dad that he's not talking to us. Is he coming back home mum?" She shook her head, unable to speak for a moment for she couldn't bear the thought of losing him.

"Dennis, dad is not very well," she replied, gently caressing my head. I could feel the weight of sadness bearing down upon her for I had never seen her like that before nor had I ever seen her cry. Our eyes met and I wished I could take the hurt and the pain away from her. It was an entirely new experience for me who thought that only small children would cry. I thought it better not to ask any more questions in case I made matters worse. The hospital was less than two hundred yards from the beach so we crossed the main road and found a cool spot in the shade of a Casuarina tree with branches that hung over us in a manner as though to say, *I understand the hurt you are carrying.* There we sat, mother and son, for a while looking out to sea. Nothing much was said but I could see that many things were whirling around in her mind. For me, just sitting there looking out to sea with mum brought back memories of the evening I lost my hat on the jetty and whether I would ever have the opportunity again to go walking on the jetty with dad or even see my hat again.

We returned home that afternoon. Dad never did. Very early the next day, a small police van drew up outside the shop. A police emerged and delivered a brown envelop to my mum. She slowly opened it with trembling fingers. It was as though she knew what was in it. There she stood transfixed to the spot for a long silent moment as though in a daze as the envelope drifted slowly to the ground. The scream that tore from her mouth ripped through the air so loudly that it brought passers-by running into the shop. Some put their arms around her to comfort her for it was as though they knew what had happened even before she had time to say. The shop was immediately closed as a matter of respect. A dead hush settled over the entire building. It was a moment of disbelief and shock. Mum sounded disoriented and looked scared. She was staring at us without seeing us. She was already feeling alone and vulnerable.

The next time I saw dad, he was lying in a box in the sitting room upstairs. I had to stand on my toes to get a good view of his face so determined was I to see him. Once again my mind was over-run with thoughts that left me feeling very sad and lonely even though I was surrounded by people. *Who is going to take me swimming on Sunday mornings or for a walk on the jetty on Sunday afternoons? Who is going to take me to church on Sunday evenings? Who is going to buy that car we saw? Who is going to play with me around the Christmas tree on Christmas mornings?* These and many more thoughts overpowered me until I was led away quietly by Lillian who saw I was having a bad time. She was told by my mum to keep me away from all that was happening as much as possible. By now there was a continuous line of people going up the outer stairs

47

to the upper floor to pay their respects. It was my first encounter with death, an experience I never forgot. It was my dad and I was only seven.

In Barbados, like in many other hot countries in those days, funerals took place within twenty-four hours. So it was with my dad. Beneath a large flamboyant tree with its bright red and creamy-yellow flowers through which the mid-afternoon sun blasted its way, he was lowered gently into his grave. Even the dry pods above which usually rattle with every passing breeze stood still for that moment as every thud of earth hitting the box sent shivers down my spine. Screams from mum, Lillian and aunt Daisy ripped through the afternoon air like when a curtain is vigorously torn apart. Soon it was all over.

The shop remained closed for some time during which friends and relatives came to see us. It was eventually re-opened and things seemed to be getting back to normal but to me things didn't look or feel the same without dad moving around in his white apron as he swept outside and inside the shop on mornings while enjoying the occasional joke with passing customers. My mum did very little in the shop. She left the bulk of the work to the attendants preferring to spend most of the time on the veranda upstairs looking out to sea. I was not allowed to go to school. Sometimes, with her hand around me, we would sit together into the twilight. It made me feel as though we had been shipwrecked together and were clinging to each other for our very survival. It felt like our hearts were sliced in two with a surgical knife. It was brutal.

Occasionally mum would be joined by Daisy, dad's sister who often came to spend a couple of weeks. Together, they would spend much time talking about dad and the plans he had. Mum knew how to look after a house and a family; she knew how to entertain and she was a source of strength for my dad, but she lacked the kind of acumen to run a business successfully. It was a weakness well known to some of her 'friends' who wasted no time in exploiting the situation by descending upon this vulnerable woman like vultures in search of what they could get. They borrowed but never repaid. Soon there was not enough to stock the shop. Shelves gradually became empty which attracted less and less customers. The shop once heaving with customers now had a mere tickle. The good days had gone. We were heading for a downfall. The next eighteen months saw mum struggling to keep the business afloat when, one very hot night in August, she entered my bedroom and sat on my bed as I was about to fall off to sleep. She drew me close to her as she always did when she wanted to prepare me for what she had to say.

"Come my child, I have something to tell you." Held in this close position, I sensed from her breathing she was about to say something terrible. Disaster had struck a second time in less than two years. I lifted my head slowly but my words came out quickly as I gazed into her eyes now red and damp.

"What is it mum? What is it?" I asked frantically. She put her hand firmly around my shoulders as we sat on the bed. I could see she was fighting back tears but a single teardrop landed on my face. Her breath caught on a sob as the hard truth tumbled out of her mouth for she was drifting between disbelief and despair.

"Son, things have happened and we have to leave the shop," she whispered, her throat tightening with unshed tears. These cold words immediately sent a chill throughout my body and put my brain in a spin.

"What happened, mum?" I asked, anxious to know what had happened to make her cry again. At this point, she rose and opened a window allowing a gentle night breeze to bring some relief from a very warm sticky night. My mind was now running hot with memories of my dad. I knew my mum was never happy after losing dad and it appeared that she had lost all interest in living for she never did anything in the shop again in spite of encouragement from Daisy and other family friends like the Carringtons from Boscobell. She couldn't see a future without my dad. Sometimes while upstairs on the veranda looking out to sea even I would try to comfort her and occasionally wipe the tears from her eyes as we sat together.

"Bad things have happened to your mum Dennis so we have to leave the shop soon."

"Why mum, why and when do we have to leave?" My body was now frozen with shock. "Soon," she said, bending gently over me.

"Tomorrow mum, tomorrow?" I said screaming and gripping her arms. "Why mum, why mum, why?" My tears burst into floods as I screamed in sheer agony. *I had not long lost my dad and now I am going to lose my friends, but I also felt very sorry for my mum.* These were some of the thoughts racing through my mind as we sat and cried together.

"Son, things have happened that you will not understand now but I am sure you will one day." Her arm was still around me. I could hear her sobbing and I did not want her to remove her arm. The grandfather's clock in the sitting room struck eight. "Try to sleep now darling," pulling the blanket gently over me. Unable to tell me anymore, she got up and left the room closing the door quietly behind her. I started to sob. I couldn't understand why we had to move. Once again, my mind was flooded with thoughts: *I will not be able to see my friends any more, especially Jack. No more playing in the back yard with him. No more climbing up*

50

the cherry tree in the yard after those dark red, sweet cherries. Will I ever go to the beach again? Will there be a beach or sand to play on? And will I be able to see little boats with white sails and big boats which, from the veranda, look so pretty at night when the lights are on? Will Lillian be coming with us and how will my brother Elliott find me? These and many more thoughts weighed down on me so heavily that I eventually cried myself to sleep.

The sun was beginning to peep through my window when I was awakened one morning by a noise from downstairs: boxes and bags were being packed and made ready for the move. Some customers and friends had come to give mum a hand and were chatting quite loudly as they went about the task. Lillian made me breakfast which I found difficult to eat for it was to be my last breakfast in that house. Gone were the happy faces as everybody seemed busy getting things together. After breakfast, I ambled off into the yard and sat quietly on the bench under the cherry tree, the very tree under which I sat with my grand-dad listening to his stories about his days in the gold fields in Guyana. I no longer wanted to play with my toy bus or car or pistol. I gazed at the back of the house without seeing anything but a dove settling on a branch in the cherry tree. It was the very dove that would often greet me with its coo as I stood at my bedroom window absorbing the sights, smells and sounds of a tropical morning. I wondered if I would again have friends like Tim and Harry from next door, or if I would ever again have the chance to dance around the maypole in their yard with our mums and dads. And what about Andrew and Cheyne who lived in Mango Lane? After a while I was joined by Lillian who, seeing I was not doing very well, put her arm around me and tried as best as she could to comfort me.

After lunch that day, with all our belongings loaded on to a truck, we set off for what to me was unknown country. Mum sat with the driver. Lillian was not coming for mum could no longer afford a maid. I was placed safely between sacks of rice, sugar and furniture at the back. Passing the cemetery where dad was buried I gazed at it until it was too far for me to see any more. Tears made their way down my cheeks like miniature rivulets. I had missed my dad and I knew then that I would never see him again. Travelling south along the main west coast road, my eyes lingered on patches of blue sea interrupted with coconut groves and houses so near to the beach that, any exceptional rise in the tide, could see them flooded with sea shells and sea urchins. Most houses were of timber, but just occasionally we would pass a stone building, maybe a hotel with white walls seemingly overrun by creeping Bougainvillea with its pink and red flowers. Sometimes too, an open space would allow me to have a fleeting glimpse of small fishing boats with their white sails bobbing up and down on the waves making their way home with their catch. I could see women (fish vendors) with large baskets assembled on the golden sandy beach awaiting their arrival. Soon we would turn inland and this fleeting coastal pageantry would be lost. By then, the intense heat of the afternoon sun had driven me to the point where I was finding it difficult to keep awake. After about thirty minutes I was awakened by my mum's call. "Come Dennis, we are here." It reminded me very much of the call she would give me at the end of Sunday service at the Methodist church.

We had arrived in Peterkin's Road St. Michael. Getting down from the truck, I suddenly realized one of my greatest fears for I looked around to find there was no sea, no sand, no boats and that there would be no sound of waves breaking on the shore or the rattle of seashells taken back to sea by receding waves. I gazed in silence, shocked and horrified at the little wooden building that was to be our new shop and home. It was a single-gabled house with an adjoining shed standing on rectangular blocks of coral limestone. The whole structure veered slightly on one side, no doubt from age. There was no upstairs, no veranda and no large backyard. What I saw was a small building with a galvanized roof so low that it was almost impossible to stand the intense heat when inside during the day and extremely difficult to sleep at night. It was a hot house too far from the sea to share any sea breezes. My whole world had collapsed and so did that of my mum.

I did not attend school for a short while although to me it seemed a year. Instead, I spent most of the time lounging around in the shade of a tamarind tree trying to understand what was happening to us but without any success. During that time, I made two friends with whom I would go walking about on afternoons for the school holidays had arrived. It was on one of these walks that I discovered Strathclyde, a district of stately homes and towering majestic royal palms lining both sides of the street. The name itself tells you it was a community of Scots who had settled there in the early days and who had done well. I was about to enter the avenue one afternoon when one of my friends shouted, "No Dennis, don't walk down that avenue." "Why not," I snapped, looking somewhat puzzled. "Rich white people live there and they have dogs and watchmen to keep you out." Here, even the street lights were different. They gave off a kind of blue/purple glow. I learnt later that they were gas lamps, not electric lights. It was a different world: a world where 'undesirables' were kept out with chains, concrete barriers and fearsome watchmen with dogs who patrolled day and night. It was a district in which the only non-whites to be seen were watchmen and servants. I did not know it at the time, but it was my first encounter with racial segregation. It was an experience with which I was not familiar. As small boys we found it difficult to understand what was going on but we always observed the unwritten code for boundaries.

7

Horrifying Days At My Second School

*L*ife in Peterkin's road was tough for me and probably more so for my mum. The building did not have enough room to accommodate a family with a small boy, especially one who was accustomed to large rooms and a large backyard. I was very unhappy and my mum knew it. What is more, I was not attending school. She soon decided that it would be better for me to live with her parents in the Ivy, a large district in the suburbs of Bridgetown. Within four weeks I was on the move again.

At the point where the road leading to the Back Ivy joins the Front Ivy, there was a two-gabled house with a small adjoining flat-roofed shed all standing on coral limestone blocks. This was the house of my mum's parents, my adopted grandparents. This was to be my new home. The smaller of the two gables at the front reflected my grandma's character. Here were some of her most treasured artefacts: a variety of multi-coloured glasses and porcelain in a mahogany cabinet. On the grey painted walls hung family pictures, some turning slightly brown with age but hanging in carefully chosen places. There were also four comfortable cane-bottomed chairs and a couch (a chaise longue), all of mahogany and adorned with white crocheted chair-backs that brought a slight touch of elegance to the room. Beneath the two front windows and on either side of the front entrance were four croton plants with their green and yellow leaves and a Pride-of-Barbados the National flower with a yellow margin around its red petals. Together they displayed an external splash of colour.

A small mahogany table took centre position in the front house. On it stood a vase around which were yet more photos. In the corner next to a window was a rocking chair. It was from this window that grandpa would sit and chat with passers-by or just watch the world as it went by: children going to and from school, red buses, the bread van, the truck with its load of soft carbonated drinks and the snowball cart pushed by its vendor and much more. It was, however, the twice weekly visit to the Ivy by a donkey-drawn cart laden with fruit and vegetables from the country (a kind of mobile green grocer) that brought grandpa the most pleasure. From this cart would come the summoning call: *breadfruit, yams, potatoes, eddoes, peas…….. come and buy*. The slightly bent and aging vendor, Mr Bracey, perched on a corner of his cart that wobbled from side-to-side, would occasionally flap the reins while slowly making his way along the Front and Back Ivy serving his customers. He would often stop for a short while to have a chat with grandpa. Without any garden large enough on which to grow anything, Mr Bracey, dressed in his slightly worn-out blue dungarees (blue jeans) and khaki shirt, was a welcomed sight to the people of the Ivy District.

The second and larger gable housed two bedrooms. In the yard was a large tamarind tree which provided welcome shade on very hot days while supplying us with large succulent fruit. The branches were strong enough to support a swing on which I was to spend much time with my friends. In the adjoining shed was the dining table and kitchen. Even without an upstairs my grandparents' house had more and better accommodation than that at Peterkin's Road. It was here that another chapter in my life was about to begin for my grandparents would now be taking over the role of bringing me up. Grandpa was a retired tram-driver who often told me interesting stories of his days when horse-drawn trams did the work of buses linking the well-to-do suburbs of Bridgetown to the town centre in the early 20th century. He would tell me stories about the two horses, Tiger and Brandy, that pulled his tram and about the many places he stopped along the way to drop off and pick up passengers. This would even include the circular motion he made with his hands when applying the brake to reduce the strain on his horses when going downhill.

Grandpa was also very good at playing draughts (checkers), a game we spent many hours playing together as we talked and joked but Friday was special for him. He was always well dressed for his journey on foot to the old tram depot in the town for his weekly pension. It was also an occasion for him to see his friends and spend some time in the rum bar. He was never drunk although he would at times find it rather difficult to keep a straight line on his way home. My smile would break into a gentle laugh when I see him in the distance making a desperate effort to keep to the side of the road but it was also a time when I could expect a supply of sweets. Grandma was short and very pleasant - a woman whose character and taste were reflected in the manner in which she kept everything around her. She would hum her favourite tunes as she went about her daily chores, one of which was to see that I was up, had breakfast and left for school on time.

St Giles Primary was a school that boasted of getting students into the top grade secondary schools of the time but it was here too that, as a boy of just eight, I was to have another bitter

Dean Alleyne

experience. It was one of physical pain and emotional distress. Every teacher carried a leather strap with which they delivered corporal punishment. These straps were used with the kind vigour and brutality that made me think teachers were competing with each other to see who could deliver a blow with the greatest impact. So inhumane was the practice that, many years after, an incoming head-teacher referred to the school as a butcher-shop and immediately banned the use of such straps by any member of staff other than himself.

On my arrival at my new school, I was assigned to class two which was split into two groups: the quick learners and the slow learners. I was put into the group of slow learners. Each group had its own teacher carrying the emblem of the school - a leather strap neatly rolled up and positioned on the teacher's table - a sight that caused fear and trembling to grip every sinew in my body. I, like many others in my group, suffered mercilessly at the hands of a teacher who, like the others, thought that power and control was in the strap, a piece of tanned cowhide about one yard in length and two inches wide. Many a time, as I stood in line awaiting my turn like a lamb to the slaughter, I trembled with fear as I saw each boy ahead of me pleading for mercy that never came. Students would scream long before the two lashes were delivered on the bare palm of the hand and with as much force as the teacher could muster. Once delivered, the poor wretches would turn to make their way back to their seats, faces screwed up, backs bent almost horizontally to the floor and hands held tightly between their legs to soothe the pain and I would feel that hurt and pain long before I had received the strap.

Like the others, I would slowly approach in fear and trembling, screaming and looking up at the teacher, my vision blurred from tears welling up and flowing down my cheeks. As he raised his arm to deliver the blow, I would sometimes try to soften it

Walking Through The Pain

by pulling my hand back a little but this often meant getting an additional one in the back for so doing. On returning to my seat, I would find it very difficult to concentrate. Tears streaming down my face would fall on the page on which I would be trying to write which was almost impossible with a swollen palm. In fact, at times both palms were so swollen that, on returning home for lunch, it was almost impossible to hold a spoon or fork. It was not for bad behaviour for such a thing was not expected of you. It was merely for not getting an arithmetical calculation correct or being unable to rehearse a times table correctly, or not being able to read as fluently as the teacher expected or even forgetting a verse of poetry or not being able to do a piece of homework. Nor was it any better for those arriving late on mornings for they would be greeted by a head-teacher standing at the door delivering hurtful blows to all late-comers, in spite of the long distance some of them would have walked to get to school.

It was the kind of experience that saw me develop a fear of school, a phobia so intense that I started to cut school on several days. On such days I would set off for school as usual but as soon as I came to the first cane field, I would look around and, satisfied that no one was about, make a mad dash for the middle of the field. There I would spend the morning or afternoon or whole day only emerging carefully on hearing the voices of other children making their way home for lunch or at the end of school. It had to be timed well to make it appear as though I was somewhere behind merely trying to catch up with a small group of boys. I had to be as quiet as possible because stepping in or out of a field of sugar cane can be a very noisy affair. Grandpa and grandma never knew what I did and I was lucky in that it never rained on any of those days for this would have forced me into the open to make a dash for shelter. It was a harrowing experience for an eight-year old lad who, within two years, had

59

Dean Alleyne

lost his dad, moved from Speightstown to Peterkin's Road, seen his mum grow more and more sad as the business collapsed and had found himself in a school where screams and cries seemed to be the order of the day.

But my time in the Ivy also had its pleasanter side for it wasn't long before I made friends with a few boys of my age among whom my closest were Neville and Dalton. School holidays would see us getting together about mid-morning and, armed with a bat and a ball, just go for walks across harvested cane fields of the Pine, a plantation less than thirty minutes-walk away. We would stop occasionally to join in any game of cricket we came across. Carrying our own bat and ball was a kind of a passport to join a game because boys always welcomed additional cricket gear and others enthusiastic enough to share their kit. Each of us had a favourite player whom we would try to imitate either through the shots we made with the bat or the balls we bowled or even the way we kept wicket. Bats were made from pieces of hardwood and balls from smaller pieces rounded and covered with tightly knitted old cloth or soft tarmac. Having had enough of the game, we would continue our meandering in search of a small fruit - 'dunk'- which grew on the thin soils of exposed craggy coral limestone in the vicinity of Clapham and Britton's Hill on the outskirts of Bridgetown. The fact that the tree had sharp prickles never deterred us so determined were we to get at the red and yellow tasty fruit. This would often be followed by a quick dash to the nearest tap by the roadside to quench our thirst brought on by the walk through intense heat and eating dunks. On Friday and Saturday nights when there was no school next day, we would spend much time under the nearby street lamp. Here we told jokes of the kind in which small boys indulged. At other times we would catch beetles attracted by the light, remove their wings and put them to race. To us it was all good fun only broken when one of us was summoned

60

in by our parents. My grandma would shout, "Dennis it's time to come in now." It only took one parent to call out and we would all disperse leaving the beetles to make their way slowly through the short grass by the roadside.

8

Mum Hits Rock Bottom

*M*um came from the shop in Peterkin's Road to the Ivy to see me on Sundays. She often cooked the Sunday meal leaving grandma free to relax and enjoy the day. She took me to the Methodist Church in Belmont Hill on Sundays as she did when we were in Speightstown. The intense heat on our return journey from church was only temporarily relieved by the smell of beef, pork or chicken stew wafted to us on a gentle breeze from the houses we passed on our way home. In Barbados it was customary to have fish during the week but meat or poultry on Sundays. Grandpa would usually be sitting in his rocker at a window greeting folk on their way to and from church. At about ten the red bus would stop almost twenty yards away from our house and, coming towards the house after the bus had gone, would be mum carrying a handbag of things needed for the coming week. My face would glow with excitement on seeing that loving smile only a mother can give. Grandpa would share my excitement by announcing, *here she comes.*

"Grandma, Grandma, here comes mum," I would shout, running around like a poodle greeting its master or mistress. An air of excitement would flood the house. It was Palm Sunday on this

63

occasion and church-goers were already making their way to St Barnabas Church about 30 to 40 minutes away on foot. Between the greetings shared by grandpa and some of the folk, I noticed my mum's smile lacked its usual sparkle as I covered the three steps in one leap in my mad rush to meet her on that particular morning. With her hand around my shoulders we walked slowly to the door. "Hello my darling, have you been a nice boy?" she asked in a hushed voice and sounding unhappy. She paused for a moment to say hello to our next-door neighbour who, like grandpa, was also in place to greet any passers-by.

"Yes mum," I replied pulling her hand more closely around my neck. As grandpa and grandma greeted her, I was already unpacking the bag frantically in search of sweets she knew I liked. But it was as though she had planned for me to unpack the bag because, by the time I found the sweets hidden at the bottom, I had placed all the other items on the table. This brought a chuckle from mum and grandma who had obviously observed the archaeological dig I had to undertake to reach the sweets. Grandpa always wanted to know how she was getting on with the shop while grandma would be occupied putting away the groceries in the cupboard. While mum busied herself preparing the Sunday meal she would also find time to probe me.

"How is school? Do you like it?" she asked with a side glance while chopping an onion. It was the unusual mild tone in her voice that triggered a wave of anxiety in me sending my mind into fast rewind. Mum was not her usual self. She looked as though something was weighing heavily on her mind. I didn't know what it was but I had seen her like this before. It was after dad died and the memories of what followed that made me wonder if something similar was about to happen. I had not yet got over my moments of distress and now the cold fingers of fear were already clutching at my heart.

"School is good mum," I replied, not intending to give her worry by telling her about my unpleasant experiences although I had the feeling that, from the unexcited way in which I replied, she knew all was not well. She did not know the physical brutality I suffered at school nor did I know that the shop in Peterkin's Road was failing. It was as though we had made a non-verbal agreement not to speak about what we were each going through. Soon, lunch was ready. Although quite unlike that I was accustomed to in Speightstown, it was a very delicious Sunday meal and one to which I looked forward very much. We talked about several things. Grandpa would tell mum how clever I was at draughts while grandma would talk about how she helped me with my homework. Mum always made us feel that things were okay at the shop although she no longer spoke with the kind of fervour to which I was accustomed. What I didn't know was that the shop at Peterkin's Road was now also running into difficulty and that very soon, she would be forced to close and say goodbye to the business of shop-keeping. After fourteen months, the shop was eventually closed and mum joined us in the Ivy not for a visit but to live permanently, an indication that yet another chapter in my young life was about to be written.

Without any real income and perhaps all savings gone, mum was now very much dependent on my grandparents' pension to live. To her, this was an almighty crash. The bottom had fallen out of her life and, although she never voiced this, it later became clear to me, even at that age, that I was becoming a burden. I knew she loved me dearly but things were getting harder and harder. It was becoming more and more difficult for her to satisfy my basic needs and to provide the simple things to which I looked forward and took for granted. For a while she tried to feign a calm until one event in particular brought it home to me that things were very bad. She could no longer afford to keep me well clothed. Our standard of living had taken a dive

Dean Alleyne

and, unlike my biological parents who grew a commercial crop — sugar cane - or who grew their own vegetables like potatoes and yams and cassava and much more, my mum did not have these to keep us going.

It was the wedding of one of her nephews which left me in no doubt that my mum had fallen on hard times. We were of course invited but on the morning of the wedding I was on the swing when she called me in and said. "Dennis, we cannot go to the church but I want you to go to the feast (reception) at the house. You can wear your blue shirt and the tie your uncle Dillon brought you when you were in Speightstown. You can also wear your grey trousers." I was disappointed we could not go to the church but it became clear to me later that afternoon. As I was getting dressed, my eyes fell on a pair of partly worn out shoes in the corner, the very shoes I would be wearing. The upper parts were slowly becoming detached from the soles which were worn out in parts. I knew that mum would never have allowed this to happen. In fact, so bad was the situation that, in the absence of boot polish, she rubbed them with the peel of a banana to make them look clean. I had nothing else to wear apart from the battered sandals I wore to school. *How am I going to get pass my friends and their mums and dads who will be there looking at everyone going into the house? They are bound to see the shoes I am wearing to a wedding, shoes with holes, top and bottom,* I pondered. I was already feeling very ashamed and embarrassed as well as sorry for my mum whom I could sense felt it would have been better had we not been invited. *"What answer would she give when asked by neighbours why I was allowed to go to a relative's wedding wearing worn-out shoes?"* Though young, it played very much on my mind because I felt she was probably more distressed than me as such news would get around the district like an uncontrolled cane-fire.

I decided to use an alternative route to reach the house about one hundred and fifty yards away where the reception was held. *"I know what I will do. I will take the back lane where nobody will see me. I will cross the road quickly and dash into the house by the back gate."* The back lane from our house ran parallel to the road and eventually curved and joined the front road just opposite the house. This would perhaps have worked well except for a heavy downpour of rain minutes before I was ready to leave. It now meant I also had to navigate a muddy back lane with large puddles of water and mud. I set out through our back gate sticking closely to the overhanging canes to avoid the puddles but, in doing so, I ended up on mud patches. Add to this the water from overhanging cane drenching my shirt and you would have a reasonable picture of the sorry state I was in when I reached the house. In the end, it was difficult to tell the difference between the colour of the socks sticking out of my shoes and the shoes themselves for by then my shoes were almost entirely covered with mud. I tried as best I could to wipe them off on the grass verge before crossing the road to enter the house by the back gate. As I did so, my fear of anyone seeing me choosing this route after a heavy downpour instead of the front road made me cry. I had to position myself in a way that would not attract my friends' attention to my worn-out shoes. I did not enjoy the occasion. Life for my mum and me continued on a downward spiral until one day my biological mother turned up. They had somehow got wind of what was happening and had made the decision to have me back in the village where I was born. The little lad who once had everything was now at the point of having nothing. Small though I was, I knew it ripped my mum's heart apart.

9

The Long Road Back

It was the usual bright sunny day and people were going about their daily tasks. Mr Bracey, the mobile green-grocer, was doing his usual deliveries. Further up the road to the east was the bread man with his bread cart that resembled a small gabled house on two wheels. He was doing a brisk trade with a small group gathered around the cart. The smell of freshly baked turn-overs, buns, jam-tarts, coconut bread and cake wafted on a gentle easterly breeze was enough to make my mouth water. It was the last Thursday in the summer holiday and I was sitting at the window looking out hoping that one of my friends would pass by and call. A number of buses passed, but as this one drove away, I could see quite clearly it was my mother from the country approaching with her usual basket of ground provisions on her head. I was now accustomed to seeing her once a month and, although I was excited to see her, I also wondered why she had come so soon after her last visit.

I hastily opened the louver doors and, clearing the three steps in one leap as usual, I rushed to meet her. As she got closer, we broke into smiles simultaneously: smiles that got broader and broader as she got closer and closer. Her hands were soon

69

Dean Alleyne

around me as I looked up at her while making our way to the steps. I knew she would have mangoes, cashews and other things for me. In the few moments it took us to get up the steps and into the house, we had exchanged the kind of greetings shown only between a loving mother and a son. With the basket now safely on the dining table, both mothers began to unpack the 'goodies' from the country: potatoes, yams, cassava, limes, peppers, okras, fruit and lots more, while exchanging pleasantries. I was quick to seize one of the juicy mangoes from the table.

"How is Stanley and what is he doing now the crop season is over?" asked mum.

"Oh, he is alright," replied my mother, removing the hatpin from her light brown hat and allowing her long dark hair to fall freely.

"I left him getting ready to plant some cassava." She went on to explain what was happening in the village and how my grandparents and my brothers were doing. My biological father always made it a point of seeing me at least once a month but he probably felt that my mother was better suited to handling what was to take place. He couldn't witness the pain my mum would be going through in such a situation.

"I heard there was quite a lot of rain in St Andrew recently. How did you all fear?" asked my mum. Conversation did not flow as freely between them as I had witnessed before for it seemed as though my mum was finding it difficult to find something to talk about. This was most unusual for she was a very good conversationalist. She was feeling distressed that things had got so bad with us that she would have no option but to let me return to the village. She no doubt felt she had failed me and my late dad and, even as she spoke, her eyes revealed the depth of her sorrow.

Walking Through The Pain

"A few bridges were washed away including the one leading to Turners Hall Wood. I don't know why they don't build a proper bridge there instead of a stupid little thing of wood that shakes when you cross it," my mother replied while enjoying a jam puff and a cold glass of ginger beer. It was known for some time that the deep clay soil on which the bridge was built could not withstand the erosive power of the river when in flood. "They have put two very heavy wooden planks down so you can cross until the bridge is repaired," she added. By now grandma who had joined the conversation had returned to her dusting and re-arranging of the front room. A light easterly breeze had funnelled its way between our house and our neighbour's to dislodge a couple of doilies on the chair backs. I had joined grandpa in a game of draughts near his favourite window through which my attention was occasionally drawn to a humming bird darting between the red and yellow flowers of the Pride-of Barbados, a plant grown in almost every front garden because of its beauty. This gave my mum and my mother an opportunity to chat.

"It's your turn to play little Dennis," grandpa reminded me now more pre-occupied with trying to work out why my mother had visited us again so soon, than concentrating on the game in hand. I was just about to make what was my cleverest move on the board when my mum called out quietly, "Dennis, come here son." My head and shoulders made a sharp ninety degrees turn. I hastily made my way to her and, with both hands on my shoulders, she looked down at me with a half-smile. "Would you like to spend some time with your mother in the country? You will see your brothers, especially Elliott as well as your father, your cousins, your uncles and aunts and your other grand-dad." Her voice trailed off as she bit back a sob.

"Yes mum." I didn't know whether to be sorry or glad, for I didn't want to upset either of them. My mother expressed her joy with

71

a quiet smile while mum's face, though not rigid, lacked that look to which I was accustomed. Even then I could see she was hurting for she had not quite succeeded in masking the anguish. It would be the first time I was leaving her for an extended period, how long, I didn't know, nor did she. They had obviously worked out that, seeing what I had already gone through, it would be better not to tell me my stay would be a long, long one.

"But you will have to take some things with you: things like your toys and the three reading books and your colouring pencils and writing book," she added before disappearing for a short while into the bedroom, giving me a chance to chat with my mother. It was as though mum felt we should have a little time together.

"Is it far from here that we are going?" I asked now very eager to see my grand-dad and my brothers.

"Yes, my son and we will have to leave soon because we have to take two buses to reach home before dark." The words *'before dark'* got me thinking.

"Why before dark? Are there no street lights?" I asked anxiously and with slightly squinted eyes.

"No Dennis, we have no electric lights and that is why we have to leave soon." I was still trying to work out what it would be like without electric lights when mum returned with a brown paper bag neatly tied. In it were my clothes, books and toys.

"I have put some of your toys in the bag for you," said mum in a trembling voice while touching the four corners of the brown parcel to make sure it was secured. It was a sign of nervousness for it seemed as though she was hardly conscious of what she was doing.

Walking Through The Pain

"Did you put in my little bus too?"

"Yes, I have," she said softly and then her eyes met mine. Everything she felt for me was in her eyes. It was mid-afternoon and, from the way my mother was tidying her basket, it was clear that we would soon be leaving. I looked at the Tamarind tree and the swing which gave me and my friends so much fun and at the small two-door shop next door where I often bought sweets and roasted peanuts. I walked slowly to the far corner of the back house where I kept my bat and ball and held them in my hands for a moment. I began to hurt inside for somehow I felt this would be a long spell away from my mum. After a change of clothes, I was ready for the journey: one that would bring a host of new and strange experiences.

"Come my son," said my mother, "we have to go now so say bye to your mum, grandpa and grandma. We don't want to miss the 4 o'clock bus from town." I walked over slowly to grandpa and grandma who held me and kissed me. They must have known this was going to be a very long holiday because I could see tears in their eyes.

"Have a nice time with your brothers and cousins," said grandma in a trembling voice as she turned and walked away slowly to take some washing off the line in the back. She could take it no longer. With my little packet of clothes safely tucked under my arm, mum held me close to her, so close that I could almost feel her pain with every beat of her heart. I looked up and as I did so, tears streaming down her face, were beginning to settle on mine. It was only the approaching bus that caused us to release each other. It was that very red bus that had passed by our window many times before. On reaching the bottom of the coral stone steps, I looked back and, with my little face now awash with tears, I saw my mum wave gently and say softly between

73

sobs while blowing her nose, "Now you be a nice boy, hear." I could see her gazing at the bus until it disappeared around the corner.

It was a sad day for me, my mum and my mother who also shared my hurt. I was again at the start of a journey into the unknown. As the bus turned left from the Ivy Road into Howell's Cross Road, we passed the house of one of my friends. Neville and Dalton were sitting on the front step with a bat and a ball no doubt expecting me to join them in a game of cricket on the nearby pasture later. I waved at them slowly but they did not wave back. They simply stared at me in astonishment for I was sitting on the bus next to someone they had never seen before. As the bus made its way along Howell's Cross Road, sad thoughts crowded my mind. *"When will I see them again? I will miss going for walks with them or playing cricket on the pasture near the Erie Great house or racing beetles under the street light at night or going dunk scrumping."*

Passing another little shop which we often visited for sweets and buns, it suddenly dawned on me that this holiday could be longer than I was thinking. It was the first time I would be away so long from my mum and I knew I would miss her very much but I also knew she was already missing me. I began to sob. My mother drew me closer to her in an effort to comfort me. Within twenty minutes we were in Roebuck Street with its large shops belching out the smell of salted cod and salted beef which, when combined with that from fruit and vegetables in street vendors' large trays, brought back memories of my days in Speightstown.

Small bakeries filled the air with the sweet smell of freshly baked bread. Within a few minutes we were passing the Parliament Building with its large clock, the chimes of which governed the movement of buses out of the bus stand located between the

Parliament Building and the careenage. The careenage was the more sheltered part of the little harbour in which schooners with their tall masts would be anchored. It is here that Constitution River empties into the Caribbean Sea. But before I could soak up the full effect of my surroundings: the river, the boats and the Parliament Buildings, we were off the bus and making our way down Broad Street to the lower bus stand to take the blue bus to a far-away place: a place unknown to me.

It reminded me of those days when my mum would take me to town. With my hands in hers, we would meander our way through the hustle and bustle of Swan Street and other narrow side streets. Sometimes we would pass near the Careenage with stacks of imported lumber piled so high that, in my childish imagination, they looked like a range of low-lying hills. To me, a small boy, Bridgetown was always exciting with something new to see on every street so whenever my mum said, *"Let's go to town,"* I could not contain my excitement at the thought of the mysteries and joys awaiting me around every corner.

Along Broad Street, buzzing with its Thursday shoppers, we passed large department stores and small shops with shoes, clothing, household stuff and much more. Down the side streets, I could see women sitting on low stools with large baskets or trays selling fruit and vegetables. Occasionally, on passing a drugstore, we would be treated to the sweet smell of perfumes, a temporary respite from the pungent odour oozing from partly open drains by the roadside. We made our way through crowded sidewalks, through the ringing of bicycle bells, tooting car horns, donkey-drawn carts and push-carts, all competing for limited space on the streets. In all this, I felt that no one cared about the agony this little boy of eight and a half was going through. No one seemed to know or care that I was leaving my mum for the first time and that I might never see her again.

| Dean Alleyne

After another fifteen minutes we were in the lower bus-stand dominated by a huge tree providing welcome shade to the vendors from the blazing sun. I learnt much later that it was a tree much older than most things in Barbados. Less than one hundred yards away I could see a church. "That is St Mary's Church," said my mother seeing that it had caught my attention. It was a Georgian building and believed to be the oldest consecrated ground in Barbados. In the bus stand, vendors carrying on their heads trays of small packets of roasted nuts, sweets in a variety of colours, sugar cakes or oranges vied with each other for custom. There were also the mauby vendors each with a large container of ice cold mauby perched precariously on their head. Each would demonstrate her skill by holding the glass at eye level and getting the ice cold drink to flow directly from the tap above into the glass without spillage. What this miniature waterfall did was to give the drink a large foamy head, a sight very appealing to the appetite. I was also overtaken by the large collection of buses of different colours showing different signs as to where they were going: those marked Hillaby Village were blue and white; those marked Speightstown were red which I was accustomed to seeing.

"Come Dennis, we are going on that blue and white bus over there marked Hillaby. We were just about to join those boarding when we discovered it was full and about to leave. This meant waiting an hour for another one which eventually arrived to a large group of waiting passengers some with large empty baskets in which they had brought provisions from the countryside to be sold in town. Once parked, there was an immediate rush to get aboard. My mother held me very tightly as she forced her way into the bus with her small basket and me in tow. It was hazardous, as a child could be crushed mercilessly if caught in such an avalanche of large baskets driven on with a force generated by women whose sole intent was to get a seat. This skirmish was fought out particularly in the two long seats at the back and was accompanied with a kind of heated language not fit for the ears of a little chap. Anybody not carrying a large basket would think twice before attempting to secure a seat at the rear of the bus for to do so would be at your peril. Such was the drama that greeted me on the second leg of my journey to the country.

As we sat waiting for the bus to leave, it was bombarded on all sides by vendors egging passengers on to make a last-minute purchase of nuts, sweets or fruit. My mother bought me a pack of nuts and some red and white candies which I enjoyed very much on the journey. It was a tight squeeze for me as I sat there waiting for the bus to go. "When are we leaving?" I asked, sucking my candy slowly for I was now eager to get on the way. "Very soon now because the bus is full," she replied with her basket and my small parcel on her knees.

The big clock on the Parliament Building struck four. Buses started to rev up. It was a sound I had never heard before: so many buses with various sounding engines revving up in readiness to go. Soon we were on our way along Lower Broad Street, Tudor Street and Baxter's Road, leaving behind the hustle and bustle of Bridgetown. It provided a kind of momentary excitement for me as I gazed at the different shop windows and stores on our way, all displaying different but eye-catching advertising boards. None attracted me more than that I saw in the window of a large bakery - a fully clad baker nodding his head gently while pointing to a large loaf held on a small tray in his hand. Add to this the sweet smell of bread and you will understand why this grabbed my attention so much.

Such rapt attention was only broken by my mother trying to dip into her purse for the fare to give to the conductor who stood precariously on the running board with an outstretched arm.

Dean Alleyne

Soon we were passing through what my mother said was Eagle Hall, Jackson and Shop Hill. From this height, I was able to look back and view for a moment the scenery we were leaving behind: a wide expanse of land, a natural terrace all green with fields of sugar cane dotted here and there with clumps of small houses. It was a scene soon to be replaced with brown open fields nearby from which sugar cane was recently harvested. In the distance ahead of us was a large building with a chimney that belched out massive columns of black smoke. "What's that?" "That's a sugar factory," replied my mother, "there is where canes are crushed and made into sugar."

The coming and going of large trucks, some with sugar cane and others with bags of sugar bound for the port, helped me to understand what was going on there. Furthermore, the smell of boiling cane juice filled the air and brought back memories of the sweet boiled juice my uncle Dillon would often bring me in Speightstown. This factory held my attention until it was well out of sight and, by that time, this miniature prairie-like picture of wide open harvested brown fields was in turn soon replaced by one of lush vegetation: a mixture of tall fruit trees like breadfruit, mangoes, golden apples, coconut and many more, as well as lush green grass clinging to the slopes of a shallow valley through which ran a small stream. As the bus descended one slope and up the other, we were bombarded with overhanging branches laden with a variety of fruit: branches so heavy with fruit and hanging so low as to bang on the top of the bus as we drove pass. I drew nearer to my mother for I was beginning to feel a bit chilly. It being high up, the air was cooler than that in the Ivy or Speightstown. Yet, picturesque though this was, it did not stop me having certain thoughts like, *"Where are we going? Where is my mother taking me? When are we going to get there?"*

10

Scary Moments

*M*y mother took an orange from her basket, peeled it and gave me half. "We'll soon be in Hillaby Dennis, not far to go now." After ten minutes, we were at the end of the journey by bus and most of the women with large baskets were already off the bus. The sun, now hanging low in the west, was fast disappearing as is common in the Caribbean where it can seem to suddenly drop below the horizon. We were now in Hillaby, the highest village in Barbados, situated on the upper slopes of the highest point - Mount Hillaby - just over 1100 feet. As my mother helped me off the bus our eyes met. "Are we here? Is this where we are going?" She gave me a motherly look hoping it would help to prepare me for what she was about to say. "No, we are not there yet son. We now have to walk a bit before we get home." My spirits fell for I was getting hungry and hoping we had arrived.

She put the small basket on her head. This time it was not packed with groceries from the shop like in Speightstown. Instead, it had things she had bought in Bridgetown on the way to the bus that afternoon. With my small packet of clothes safely tucked under my arm, she held my hand as we set off on our next leg of the

79

journey, one that was to last more than an hour and on foot. Descending the slope of a valley and ascended the other with small chattel houses clinging to both slopes, I could see columns of blue smoke rising from kitchens. I later learnt from my mother that the evening meal was being prepared for the family but especially for those who were out working all day in the fields under the hot sun. On reaching the other side of this valley, which stands at about 850 feet, we were completely exposed to the continuous blasts of Atlantic on-shore winds from the east. My mother, seeing I was somewhat uncomfortable, took a large cloth from the basket and wrapped it around me.

"Look Dennis, can you see over yonder?" She pointed away in the distance below us to what looked like a very large black mass.

"Yes, I can see, but what is that black thing in the distance," I asked keeping the cloth securely tucked around me as I trotted along beside her while struggling to keep my balance on an uneven surface.

"That is Turners Hall Wood and we have to pass there to get home." That did not help for the sheer distance we had to walk and the massive dark blob through which we had to pass, together with a wind that seemed determined to skin me alive, drove fear throughout my body. We continued at a steady pace, nothing much was said for a while. Maybe it was because I was too busy trying to keep warm or because my mother was concerned about getting me home as quickly as possible for the lengthening evening shadows were giving way to a complete dull greyish colour. Occasionally the silence would be broken by *"hello Alice, is that your little boy?"* *"Yes, hello"* my mother would reply. *"It's getting dark, get home safely,"* would come from someone sitting at a window as we passed. It was a quick exchange repeated several times as we made our way. Just occasionally too we would be greeted by an older man making his weary way home with his small flock of sheep or a cow and carrying a large bundle of cut grass on his head as he left the world to darkness and to us.

"It will soon be night Dennis so we have to make some speed to get through the wood." The walk was not strenuous because it was all downhill so far but soon we were off the main road and on to a stony lane with large clumps of grass bursting through between partly submerged boulders exposed by erosion from surface flow of heavy tropical downpours. There were no houses, only fields of sugar cane on both sides of this very narrow uneven road just wide enough for a horse-drawn cart to pass. That dark mass, the massive blob my mother had pointed out to me earlier, was getting closer. It was Turners Hall Wood and I was having my first close-up view. Our only way home was through that dark mass of trees. By now, the sun had fallen behind the surrounding hills and was about to leave us for good. In a few minutes we would be in total darkness. I was concentrating on this dark wood ahead of us when suddenly I could hear a heavy roar which, together with the fast approaching darkness and the wood, sent a chill throughout my body similar to that I experienced at my dad's funeral. "What's that noise?" I snapped looking around anxiously and tripping over a boulder in the process.

"It is a river, my son and we have to cross it to get to the other side and then go through the wood." This was all new to me because I had never seen a river before and it was raging from heavy rainfall during the day. To make matters worse and even more daunting, I looked down to see what looked like two very large planks of wood lying flat across a rushing torrent of muddy water about twelve feet below us in a deep ravine. We paused for a few moments. I looked at the woods, the river, the two planks and then at my mother. Oh, how I wished then that I was back in the Ivy with my mum. There was no other person around. My mother looked at me with an expression that seemed to say *I am sorry my son.* I looked at her, fright transfixing me to the ground, for just then a dreadful thought gripped me: *What would happen if I slipped? There is nothing to hold on to.* My mother made sure the basket was safely perched on her head before holding me firmly by the hand with my little parcel under the other arm. As soon as she stepped on the planks they started to shake whereupon I dug my heels in like an unwilling donkey and started to scream. Nothing my mother said or did could get me to move. I could see she was very worried, but what could I do? I had never come this close to a river let alone a raging torrent twelve feet below me and over which I had to cross on two horizontal shaking planks and then enter a dismal, gloomy wood.

My mother paused. Nothing was said for a long moment. Eventually she had an idea. *This has to work because there is no one else around to help us*, she thought now looking very desperate. After forcing my little parcel into her basket, she bent forward slightly. "Come on son, get on my back, hold on tightly and close your eyes as tightly as you can," she suggested with a beseeching look. It was quite different to having a swim on the back of my dad when I was in Speightstown. I did as I was told and we proceeded to navigate our way across this unstable structure that swayed with every step she took. Although it was no more than eight feet across it felt as though we were crossing for quite some time but I knew we had crossed when my mother gave a big sigh of relief as I slid slowly from her back. "You can open your eyes now," she said. This I did and there was just enough light left that allowed me to see that smile of contentment and satisfaction written all over her face. It was the

Walking Through The Pain

smile that only a mother could give in a situation like this. All was well that ended well. What a torrent? What a mother?

With my feet now on firm ground again, we set off through the dark wood along a narrow winding path. I expected something to leap out at us at any time with every step. It was a dreadful silence and one that triggered horrible thoughts, for running through my mind were lots of *'supposes'* and *'what ifs'* and a series of horrible images only a little boy can conjure up when caught in the dark in unknown territory. My mother seemed to know every bend, twist and turn. It was as though she had a special pair of eyes, a pair quite different to mine because I was finding it difficult to see beyond my outstretched arm. I held on to her tightly closing my eyes for fear of seeing something horrible, for what would happen if something suddenly leapt out of the dark and snatched me away. We were now deep into the woods and making good time. Suddenly there was a rustling movement close to us in the undergrowth and howling sounds in the treetops above. "What's that?" I snapped, without reducing the pace at which I was walking.

"They are monkeys. We can't see them but they can see us from the treetops." This made me more scared and confused. Scared because of the sounds and confused because I could not understand how they could see us and we couldn't see them. The canopy of treetops overhead was so closely entwined that it was difficult to see the stars in the clear tropical night sky let alone monkeys.

"But will they jump on us?" I asked in fear and trepidation. It was almost too much for a young lad brought up with street lights to be suddenly thrown into the midst of a dark wood, a kaleidoscope of darkness triggering off waves of panic with any rustle in the undergrowth or sound from overhead.

83

Dean Alleyne

"No, they won't, they don't do that." This episode was followed by more swift movement in the undergrowth from time to time forcing me to ask again and again what it was, but my mother would always come up with the kind of answer intended to reduce my fear. I later learnt they were raccoons or mongooses foraging for food. The woods seemed cold and damp to me an urban youngster and, with no street lights, I would occasionally stumble over a small fallen branch or hit a patch of soggy leaves or even step into a puddle. It was also my first experience of that cacophony of sound produced by crickets and croaking frogs wrapped in the smell of a humid jungle. It was an experience that stayed in my memory. Such invisible scenes and sounds infused with the smell of a damp tropical wood only came to an end when my mother suddenly reduced her pace.

"Look Dennis, there is a light over yonder. We'll soon be out of the woods now. Can you see it?" My eyes moved into action piercing the darkness like laser beams to reveal a small light occasionally blocked out by the gentle sway of branches.

"Yes, yes I see it, I see it. What is it?" I asked, the words leaving my mouth in a jerking manner.

"That's where we are going. It is your great aunt's house," she added.

"My great aunt, who is a great aunt?" I asked bouncing along beside her, my fear subsiding as the light got closer. She probably knew that the word great aunt would not have meant much to me.

"Well," stringing out the word for a short while, "she is your grandmother's sister."

"Oh" I said in a quiet voice, not understanding what she was

84

saying. "You mean I have two grandmothers?" I asked in wonderment for it seemed as though she had tried to explain something with something even more difficult. I had already accepted that I had two mothers but two grandmothers as well! She did not reply because she felt I would soon come to understand. It was the first time I had opened my eyes for quite a while and from here on I kept them firmly focused on that single light. We were soon out of the woods and standing outside the open door of my great aunt. There she stood tall in the doorway slightly blocking the glow of an oil-burning lamp that flickered whenever a light night breeze stole its way through a door or window. It was the very light I had seen before in the distance. Not only was it the first light I had seen for some time, it was also the first house on emerging from the wood. From here, the road curved to form a large crescent about halfway up a slope. On the downside was only one large house, my grandparents' and on the upper side, a few were strung out along the side of the road with several others dotted higher up. I was able to tell this from the position of the lights.

The way this tall woman stood silhouetted in the doorway told me she was expecting us. She knew me but I didn't know her. She hugged and kissed me while admiring the outfit I was wearing but, seeing I was slightly chilly, gave me a cup of hot milk. After a brief chat we were off again. The next stop would be the house of my grandparents. Here too lived two of my aunts, one uncle and two cousins. Though it was dark I could still make out that this house was a lot larger than my great aunt's. It had two large gables, a large four-hip and an adjoining flat-roofed shed. It was clear that they were expecting us for as soon as I entered the door I was immediately mobbed by my two aunts who smothered me with kisses and wanted to know all about me. They no doubt were well aware of what my mum and I had gone through during the last two years. I looked at everyone wondering who they were for, except for grand-dad, I had never seen them before.

A screeching noise drew my attention to a bedroom door opening slowly and through the dim light of an oil burning lamp, I could see another tall elegant woman emerging. Grandma, like her sister my great aunt, was also tall, dark and slender. She was wearing a white apron reaching down to her ankles and a colourful head-tie, truly Ashanti. I had never seen her before and yet I knew she was my grandmother. Grand-dad was sitting at the window with his feet in a basin of warm water. It was his custom after a day on the farm to soak his feet in warm water perhaps to reduce the tiredness. He was gazing outside at what, I didn't know, because it was very dark. I knew him well for he would often visit me in Speightstown where we had spent much time sitting together under the cherry tree chatting. He was just about to dry his feet when I ran to him and, as if expecting me to do so, had positioned himself to receive me on his knees. I did not disappoint him. It was a moment of great joy. I was now feeling more comfortable. It was like my fist day at Speightstown primary school when, seeing my friend Jack, made me feel happy and more comfortable. Grand-dad asked me about my friends and I asked him about his horse, the one he would sometimes ride when he came to see me.

Just then a little brown dog came and sat beside us. "This is Bruce," he said gently stroking the little creature on its head. I was soon to learn more about this little fellow within the next six months of my return to the village. It was the first time I was accompanying my grand-dad to his farm and of course Bruce was in attendance. He knew the way well and often disappeared for a while into a thicket in the distance to forage but would always re-join us later wagging his tail indicating that he was successful. It was on this trip that once again I could hear a bubbling noise not far away. Grandpa turned to me with a fatherly smile. "Now you watch carefully and see what Bruce is going to do when we reach that large rock in the distance" he uttered, pointing to a large rock partly overgrown with brushwood. I was staring at him with a curious look when, on reaching the rock, Bruce made a sudden dash for the pool below the rock into which plunged a mini waterfall. Here he swam around five times before re-joining us shaking the water from his coat. Grandpa went on to describe how he did it every morning on his way to the farm and every evening on his way back.

It was a warm welcome from a family most of whom I had never seen. After about half an hour of hugs, kisses, questions and conversation, grandmother observed I was getting sleepy for it was as though two small weights were bearing down on my eyelids. "I think you better get this little fellow home now Alice, he is probably tired and sleepy," she suggested gently stroking my head. "Dennis, say bye to everybody and let's get home now," said my mother, again placing her basket neatly on her head and stretching out an arm to receive me. As we continued along this crescent-shaped road, I found it difficult to understand how people could live without street lights. This was a very great shock to a little lad who had known street lights all his life but I refrained from asking my mother why there were none. By that time, I was too tired and sleepy anyway to ask any more questions. Within minutes we were at the bottom of a very gentle slope when my mother made a sharp right turn. We had arrived. Two steps made of limestone blocks took us into a small dimly lit house made up of two medium size gables standing on wooden posts and large limestone blocks. It was the house where I was born. It was the final leg of a three-hour journey of unforgettable experiences.

The oil lamp on the small table near the window flickered from

Dean Alleyne

a slight draught caused by the opening door. Kip the little black and white dog greeted my mother in his usual way while trying to become acquainted with me. I was warmly greeted by my father whom I also knew very well but I had to be introduced to my younger brother Frank whom I had never heard of or seen before. My older brothers Calvin and Elliot were not yet home. Close to a window on the east side of the room was a large table covered with a flowered oil-skin table cloth on which stood a small tray with four turned-down drinking glasses and a water jug. The window had a ledge jutting out on which stood a large clay container with a spout. My father, seeing it was the first thing to attract my attention, remarked, "That's a monkey and it keeps water cool". I was bewildered because I just could not relate what he said to what my mother told me while walking through the wood not long ago. My father went on to explain that it was made from clay and why it was called a monkey. Clay containers kept water cool throughout the day in the days before the arrival of the fridge in Barbados. Feeling a demonstration was necessary he got a glass and poured some water. I am not too sure I heard what he was saying let alone understood for by that time I was very tired and sleepy from the journey. After a cup of hot chocolate and a piece of home-made coconut bread I was safely tucked into bed. I had come full circle.

11

A New Dawning

A dawn chorus struck up by cockerels signalled the onset of my first day in the village as I lay in bed pondering what morning would look like in my new home. Not far away were the memories of Speightstown and the Ivy District except that I would no longer be hearing Lilian's footsteps coming up the stairs to wake me up for breakfast and school or grandma opening the door and giving me a call when I was racing beetles with my friends under the street lamp at night. Here there was no cherry tree outside the window to break the incoming early morning sun rays. Instead, I was briefly entertained by the crowing of cockerels announcing the oncoming of dawn, quite a normal thing in the country. It lulled me off to sleep again only to be awakened later by the brilliant rays of the rising sun peeping through crevices of well-worn shutters and settling gently on my face. It seemed as though the sun was saying, *rise and shine, welcome to your new home* while I wondered what kind of world awaited me.

Anxious to satisfy my curiosity I jumped up, yawned, rubbed my eyes and briskly threw open the half-worn wooden shutters to be greeted with a country air I had never before experienced. It was air infused with the soft aroma of green grass and broadleaf vegetation now covered with dew drops which shone like crystals under the morning sun. It took some time to allow this feeling, that first experience to penetrate my body. The picture unfolding before me was a collection of fruit trees: mango, breadfruit, coconut, pawpaw and tamarind, their leaves slightly ruffled by a very gentle morning breeze creeping up the valley and all displaying shimmering shades of green. In the distance, I could see small columns of blue smoke rising from outdoor kitchens just like those I had seen the evening before after getting off the bus in Hillaby Village, only this time it was an indication that breakfast was on its way.

I was standing by the window in sheer awe and amazement, for I didn't think there was a world different to that I had in Speightstown or the Ivy District, when my attention was broken by the flip-flopping sound of sandals. "Morning my son and how are you feeling this morning?" It was not Lillian nor was it my mum. It was my mother approaching with outstretched arms to hug me. "It's a lot different to where you lived before, isn't it?" she said, pointing out the types and names of the various trees around us. She was obviously doing her best to make me feel comfortable in my new home. "I'll get you some breakfast," she added before disappearing into the kitchen.

I was so taken in by this panorama that, were it not for an unusual sound coming from fifty feet away to the right, I would not have noticed the large animal tethered beneath a tree: a cow lying on a bed of dried sugar cane leaves and quietly chewing its cud. Not far away and also tethered to the lower trunk of a sugar-apple tree were two pigs whose grunting and sustained trampling of the mud beneath them suggested they were anticipating their first feed of the day. It was customary to find a pig at almost every house. They were reared to provide cash when sold to a butcher or when butchered at home. The advantage was that they grew very fast and could be changed into cash within eighteen months.

In the cellar beneath the floor, a small flock of sheep were bleating indicating their readiness to be taken to the pasture. It was the kind of drama repeated at almost every house in the village. Kip, the dog, was busy chasing a cat up the nearby tamarind tree with loud barking while my mother was collecting freshly laid eggs from her brood of hens. But it was the aroma from freshly roasted coffee beans floating through the house that suggested my mother had already prepared breakfast for my father who had already left on his push-bike for work at the sugar factory. Breakfast for my father was usually a large jug of coffee and bread made from cassava flour garnished with homemade butter from cow's milk. It was a morning very different to any I had ever experienced in Speightstown or the Ivy. It was my first morning in the countryside and in the little village of my birth.

My younger brother Frank was already up and getting ready to take the small flock of six sheep to the pastures in the hills about a mile away. Apart from rising columns of smoke from other houses in the village, I could also see girls and young women carrying out one of their daily chores which was to fetch buckets of water on their heads from the village stand pipe for use during the day. Not far away, older women were busy sweeping and doing a general tidy-up of the area around their houses using coconut brooms made from the leaves of the coconut tree and very good for cleaning rough surfaces. Others, each wearing a head tie or a worn out straw hat and each carrying a hoe, were making their way to plantation fields. Men, with hoes and forks on their shoulders, were also setting out to the fields for another day's work under a hot tropical sun and yet others were taking their cows to the pastures. It was all part of a daily routine repeated in many parts of rural Barbados.

Dean Alleyne

My mother was not too keen on letting me go with Frank on the first day to the pastures but it was perhaps that country air and the smell of coffee for my father and hot milky tea and home-made bread for us, that triggered a strong desire in me to accompany him. It was my entry into a new world: a world I had never dreamed of or knew existed. It was a world for which I was not prepared but anxious to see. I wanted to see what Frank had to do so, with the sheep untethered, we were soon on our way to the pastures, the oldest member of the flock appearing to lead the others in single file. We followed the road for about one hundred and eighty yards before making a sharp turn by a disused windmill along a narrow tract and down a gentle slope where we crossed a small babbling brook. I was amazed by the way these animals were able to pick partly submerged boulders and jump from one to the other to make their way across. Any residue of sleep left in me was soon got rid of by a morning breeze embracing the valley slopes making me become more alert. Ahead of us in the far distance stood a small one-gabled house clinging precariously to a slope.

"Frank, who lives in that little house over yonder on the hill," I asked, pointing to the house from which light grey smoke was rising slowly above the galvanized roof and disappearing over the hill to blend with a light blue sky that formed the backdrop. It was one of a small group of houses, perhaps five, that huddled together on the leeward slope of a hill top about a mile away from the village and only reached by a dirt tract.

"That's uncle John's house and the pasture is not far from there." Like other houses, it stood on a combination of wooden posts and stones with enough room below for a flock of sheep. Less than nine yards away from the house two cows were tethered to a central post around which was an abundance of dry grass and cane leaves on which they slept. I had never seen uncle John

92

Walking Through The Pain

before who, like uncle Wilbert, was a peasant farmer. He too spent much time working his two acres of land and looking after his animals. Uncle John and uncle Wilbert were much younger than my mother and, being peasant farmers, they had certain things in common. The trousers they wore stopped about six inches above the ankle and, like many men in the village, they wore strong slippers made from disused tyres and canvas — a product of the village cobbler. Strapped to their belt was always a sheath with a knife used for cutting grass for the animals. They both paid frequent visits to our house in the evening to talk about the day's happenings in and around the village over a cup of hot chocolate or fresh lemon grass steeped in hot milk. They seemed to look to their older sister for advice and guidance on many things.

Uncle John's little house was well protected from easterly winds by a semicircle of wild cane, *pingwing*, a type of giant reed that seemed to thrive in the eastern Caribbean. In another ten minutes we were on a sloping pasture of short succulent grass bathed in morning dew. The scene across the valley slopes became even more alive with the clanging sounds of stone on iron stakes as sheep and cows were tethered on other pastures by daily visitors like us. It all reminded me very much of the coopers' hammers in the cooperage in Speightstown. "See if you can find two large stones," suggested Frank. I trotted off to return within minutes with two reasonably large ones. We had brought with us three iron stakes each. Once driven into the ground at an appropriate depth, it was to these that the sheep would be tethered. "We must stake them away from any steep bank because, if they stretch for grass too near to the edge, they might slip over and hang themselves," he admonished.

"But why must they be tied up to stakes?" I asked quite innocently. He looked at me with a slight frown as though to say *how come*

93

you don't that? But he quickly realised I was not a country boy and that this was my first day in the pasture.

"Because if we don't, they will eat the other people's crops of young peas or destroy their potatoes and yams and sweet cassava," he replied with a wry smile. Tethering animals was customary if they were not to wander off into neighbouring cultivated plots. Animals that had broken away from the stakes often made their way to the more succulent foliage instead of the usual grass. It was a situation that often set sparks flying between the owner of the crops and the owner of the animals for if captured, the owner of the animals would have to pay a fee to have them back. The more extreme person would slaughter the offending animal on the spot and he would be within his legal rights according to the laws of the land at the time. This however, rarely occurred. I was given my first lesson in animal husbandry by my younger brother: *always be very careful where you stake the animals.*

With the sheep safely tethered we were soon on our way back home. Frank got himself ready for school but my mother thought it would be better for me to remain at home with her that day so we could get to know more about each other. We talked about many things: my days in Speightstown including my first day at school when I wet my trousers out of fear of asking the teacher's permission to let me out of class. She told me the names of all my aunts and uncles and cousins before taking me to the school to have me registered to begin the next day. Frank was home at the end of school and after a cold drink and a piece of bread, we set out to the pastures once more to bring the flock home. It was then that he told me that at lunchtime which was 12 to 1 o'clock, he had to first run to the pasture and move the sheep around out of the intense heat of the noonday sun before coming home for lunch.

12

A Baptism Of Fire

After one day at home I was ready for school. With morning chores completed Frank and I set off for school about one hundred and fifty yards away at the top of a low hill where the ridge was sufficiently flat at the top to allow a school and other houses to be easily erected. Frank was two years younger than me but because our early childhood was different, his rural and mine urban, our jokes and stories tended to be different all of which helped up to strike up a good relationship straight away. It was as though he was looking for someone nearer his age with whom he could share his jokes since our two older brothers were much, much older than us. He was a spritely little fellow who often darted in and around the house with great rapidity. He made no delay in introducing me to some of his friends with whom he often played at marbles, kite flying or simply running around like boys of that age would normally do.

Unlike the other buildings in the village, the school was a combination of two large gables and an adjoining flat roof shed on either side, was built on a solid foundation of coral limestone blocks and cement. On the west and less than fifty yards away,

Dean Alleyne

the land rose to a further thirty feet offering a commanding view of the hills in the east and the shallow valleys dipping down to a broad coastal plain hugged by the Atlantic. It was from this low hill that I was taught my first lesson in Geography (known then as *nature study*). On that day, armed with blackboard, easel and chalk, the teacher took us to the top of this low hill and spent the morning pointing out and describing the surrounding hills and valleys in the distance. But the image that stuck with me the most was that of the rugged hills dipping down from Chalky Mount to the blue Atlantic and, though I did not know it at the time, it was an image and a lesson which was to stimulate my interest in Geography.

Sometime later I accompanied my brother Elliot on an errand to the little village of Chalky Mount which also sits on a ridge: a ridge composed of clay and sandstone sweeping down to the sea on the east coast. We arrived at a small one-door shop where we had a drink and some biscuits, but my attention was immediately drawn to a collection of items of various shapes and sizes displayed outside. "What are those things?" I asked Elliot giving his sleeve a sharp tug but it was obvious to the man behind the small counter that I had never seen such things before and he therefore thought a short lesson would be in place.

"It is called pottery and it is all made from clay. Come around the back with me and I'll show you how they are made. Bring your drink with you." It was quite clear to him that I was not really a rural lad and that I would therefore know nothing about it. Mr Springer was a cousin of my father who had been a potter all his life. It was a skill handed down through generations only in that part of the island where suitable clay was found. With a large lump of clay on the potter's wheel he showed me how each piece had to be shaped, groomed and designed.

"Look Elliot, there are five that look like the 'monkey' we have at home for keeping water cool." I pointed out. He nodded in agreement and was pleased to see I was so observant. "He said he is our father's cousin, is he Elliot?" I whispered, looking up at my older brother for confirmation.

"Yes he is and he is very clever," he replied.

"And I like his lemonade too," I added. At home my mother was delighted to hear about the things I had learnt that day.

East of the school was the playground beyond which was the school garden: a small patch of land where pupils were taught how to plant and care for lettuce, carrots, onions, tomatoes and other vegetables, some of which we were allowed to take home when harvested. It was usually an afternoon lesson to which we looked forward very much. About two hundred yards to the south of the school was a disused windmill by which we passed daily to and from the pastures. It was part of Cheltenham, a small plantation of thirty acres. Many years later I learned from an elderly aunt that it was owned by two of her uncles and that, when she was taken on a visit to see them at the mill, she was always told to keep away from the mill house for fear of her getting hurt. Like other plantations at the time, most of it was under sugar cane. The area around the mill soon became a favourite play area for my friends and me. Other than the school and the old windmill, the only other imposing structure at that time was the village Anglican Church which, although small, had stained glass windows and a large pipe organ that sprang into action on Sunday mornings in harmony with a congregation of church-going villagers whose voices could be heard for miles around.

On that first morning as I walked onto the playground I was

Dean Alleyne

immediately struck to find that, apart from the head teacher's children, none of the other children, including my brothers Frank and Elliot, wore anything on their feet. I was wearing a pair of sandals I had brought with me, very necessary in Speightstown and the Ivy where it was impossible to walk on hot melting tarmac surfaces without anything on your feet. Here, not even pumps were worn to protect the feet not from hot tarmac but from sharp gravel which covered the surface of roads in most outlying villages like St Simon's. But this comfort and advantage I enjoyed was brought to an abrupt end after one week when my mother looked at me apologetically and said softly, "Dennis son, I don't want you to wear your sandals to school any longer." Memories of my last days in the Ivy District came flooding back to me. *Was my mother going through similar difficult times as my mum?* I pondered. I was stunned for I had always worn sandals to school, but before I could work out a reason, she continued, "It doesn't look nice you wearing sandals and your other brothers don't."

Small though I was, I understood what she meant and how much it must have hurt her to say those words but you never questioned your parents. Instead, I did as I was told even though I knew that for a long time I would suffer intense pain for, wearing shoes or sandals all my life, had made the soles of my feet very tender. Without anything on my feet, I would often return home in the afternoon with bruised toes sustained while trying to chase my friends around the playground. Quite a long time after, I learned it was because of my parents' inability to keep us all in sandals that made my mother take that decision. I quickly conformed by joining my brothers and the other boys in washing my feet at the village stand-pipe before setting off for school. Going to school with dirty feet could invite some kind of corporal punishment from the teacher who did a daily morning inspection of hair, teeth, nails and feet while we were lined-up in the playground.

Apart from making new friends like Oswald, George, Wesley and Kelvin, my first day at school was not very welcoming. It was one I never forgot. We had just returned after lunch and the whole school was engaged in choral singing under the direction of a rather corpulent looking teacher. The belly of this rotund figure shook as he walked. We were all standing with our hands clasped and singing, except for me, for being new to the school, I was neither acquainted with the tune nor the words. Without any advance warning, I suddenly saw this burly figure leave his position on the rostrum and with his belly wobbling around like a large mass of jelly, proceed in the direction of my class. He had obviously observed from the podium that I was not singing and had decided to wake me up. Holding me by my head, he bent me over the desk and delivered two severe lashes on my back with his leather strap. It was with the kind of ferocity experienced only two weeks before at St Giles School. No account was taken of the fact that I was a new boy who might know nothing about the song. I screamed in sheer agony causing half the school to look in my direction. As he delivered his symbol of power and turned to make his way back, my older brother Elliot, standing about five feet away at the back of his class, looked back in utter horror and disgust, for by now tears were cascading down my face. I was shocked and in pain. I could see he felt my pain but could do nothing about it. What brutality! What a welcome!

Throughout this, I never forgot what my adopted dad and grand-dad always drilled into me, namely, *we want you to do your best at school because we want you to have a profession.* These words became indelible on my mind and I tried at all times to do the best I could. Even as a small boy in Speightstown I had observed how my adopted father went about his daily tasks with a sense of purpose. Within seven months I had made the kind of progress to warrant a promotion before the end of the first year. After spending two terms in class two, I was therefore promoted to class three where I coped quite comfortably. This was backed up by the prizes I received on each of the two prize-giving days while I was there. These usually took place during the last week of the Christmas term. It was an afternoon to which parents and guardians would be invited to hear speeches from the head teacher and a dignitary, usually the parliamentary representative for the parish. There would be the singing of Christmas carols and a short play followed by refreshments. It was a day on which prizes were awarded for things like good conduct, good attendance and good work. I shared in these awards.

Among my prizes one year was an English Dictionary, something I found extremely useful at secondary school and a copy of *Masterman Ready by Frederick Marryat,* which made pleasant reading for a boy of my age. It was a book I read so often that I could almost recite parts of it. It was a day too on which pupils' hand-made products (handy-craft) were exhibited: baskets, sieves, brooms etc. Mine was a toy car made from empty milk tins. My teacher thought it was such a good semblance of the real thing that he asked me to exhibit it. After the exhibition, it was bought by a mother for twelve cents. She felt her small son of five would be delighted to have it. To a little chap like me, twelve cents meant a lot in the very late forties especially around Xmas time. Quite unknown to me, this first sale of something I had made was to stimulate something deeper. It was the first sign of a young entrepreneurial spirit.

13

Oh, How They Toiled And Struggled!

St Simon's was a thriving little village of about two hundred people most of whom were labourers, about two percent carpenters and masons and a sprinkling of shopkeepers and teachers. Most houses clung to gentle slopes on both sides of the road along the crest of the ridge while others nestled in small pockets some distance from the main road and reached only by dirt paths which became mud tracts during the rainy season. But even such muddy conditions did not deter church goers on Sundays some of whom would trundle barefoot through the mud to church. The main road had a rough surface of ground-in gravel for it was only in the fifties that a layer of tar sand was first added to make it smoother. It is here that I was born, the twelfth of thirteen children, four of whom survived their first year and lived into adulthood.

My parents practiced a parenting style which differed slightly from the traditional. It was a time when it was thought that 'children ought to be seen and not heard.' Instead, they would always listen carefully to what we had to say before making a decision or passing judgment and there was always that outpouring of love and attention from them. One of my father's pieces of advice was: *let decency be your guide.* Though of humble background he paid much attention to his appearance especially when dressed for church it being one of the few occasions when most Barbadians would have a chance to display their best clothes. He was held in high esteem in the village for, although he did not have the privilege of a secondary education, he seemed to have that little bit over others of his generation in the village. He would often be asked by many for help in writing official letters like those to the local tax office. He was also the campaign manager for the member-of-parliament for the parish of St Andrew and could often be seen chairing campaign meetings. Needless to say, he was a very popular person in the village and the parish.

Crop season lasted from January to June on the island and was a busy time for everyone including father who worked at the local sugar factory. It was then that the sugar cane was harvested on large plantations as well as small peasant holdings. In addition to those working in the factory, there were those who worked harvesting the cane or on trucks transporting cane to the factory or bags of sugar to the port. It was the time when most money was made in rural Barbados for it was then that small farmers sold their crop to the sugar factory. While some worked in the factory itself, others worked loading trucks that transported sugar cane to factories or bags of sugar to the port. Everyone looked forward to this time of the year when houses could be repaired and when the carpenter's hammer could be heard banging away replacing weather-worn shingles or galvanized roofs. But it was also the time when my father would sometimes have to leave home sufficiently early to start work at midnight at the factory. This would often see him following an overgrown tract across country up and down gullies at midnight in the dark, his only relief coming on reaching the top of the last gully when he would see the factory lights in the distance.

Sugar cane requires a lot of attention during the weeks of early growth. It was hard work preparing the soil for young cuttings and for my father, like other small farmers, it meant spending all day in the hot sun turning the soil. After the planting, unwanted weed had to be removed and fertilisers added all of which my father did with the help of paid workers. Nor was the harvesting any less strenuous for he was often there giving a helping hand to hired workers who actually cut the canes leaving young women to carry them in bundles on their heads to a convenient place to be collected by a truck for the factory. It was the period preceding the mechanisation of sugar cane harvesting in the island and so the whole process from start to finish was a back-breaking job sometimes in temperatures exceeding thirty degrees centigrade. My father would often return home in the evening with his clothes fully saturated with sweat.

Crop time also saw my father engaged in the harvesting of another cash crop: arrowroot, a crop grown in tropical countries for its root. The powder produced from the root is used as a thickener in recipes or for medical purposes. Processing the root however required plenty water and so father always planted his crop in the plot of land nearest to the stream. On the day before grinding, my older brothers would spend hours hauling water in buckets from the river to fill two large barrels. My father and one of my uncles would take it in turns to feed the locally made mill with the root. The grinding mechanism was made up of a medium size drum around which was fixed a large version of a very course grater attached to which were two handles. Two men, usually my uncles, turned the grinding drum while others washed the root in preparation for grinding. Soon, my mother and grandmother would be bending over two large barrels using large cloths through which they would squeeze the milky juice from the pith. It was back-breaking work which sometimes engaged up to eight people.

The whole process often took about four hours and was also seen as a social occasion, a time for catching up with the latest gossip. The only payment helpers expected was a generous helping of corned beef and biscuits together with bottles of rum, lemonade and mauby. To me it seemed as though there was a group moving around the village offering help during the arrow root harvesting season. Frank and I always looked forward to such an occasion. It was fun time for us for, together with a couple of our cousins or friends, we spent much time playing in the field from which the arrowroot was harvested or catching crayfish in the nearby stream. We always looked forward to those generous servings of corned beef, biscuits and lemonade. Mother always looked after the last stage in the process when the solid starch would be cut out of large barrels and put out on large cloth sheets to be dried before eventually being sold to bulk buyers.

During 'hard-time' - July to January - the period following the crop season, my father worked as a rock blaster providing boulders for road construction. Dotted on the landscape were large mounds of coral limestone often overgrown with sage that grew on the thin soil which settled within hollows on these gigantic rocks, some the size of a two-storey building. He would spend much time using a heavy steel drill to bore a narrow hole in the rock into which he would then sink a stick of dynamite. At the sound of a whistle or a loud prolonged shout, wildlife and workers alike in nearby fields would dash for cover for such warnings would rapidly be followed in minutes by a blast loud enough to be heard for miles around and strong enough to shatter the rock or part of it. He would then use a sledge to break the large blocks into manageable pieces, boulders. Soon, two or three workers perched on large stones, would use heavy hammers to smash these boulders into smaller bits. It was hard work, it was hot and it was sweaty. Except for lunchtime when my mother would arrive carrying a basket with food, all day the air would resound with the sound of hammers and sledges going bang, bang, clang, clang. The only relief came from a cool easterly sea breeze creeping up the shallow valley. As the setting sun casts long shadows on the landscape, with his hat soaked through with sweat and clothes covered in a thin white film of dried salt, my father would make his weary way home.

My mother was much shorter, slim with black hair reaching down to her elbows. She was of mixed race for my grandfather was of Scottish descent and my grandmother of African, more precisely of the Ashanti tribe in Ghana. My mother was petite, but had a certain command of the family. She anchored it and, like many other mothers, she never went out to work for, in those days, that was seen as a husband's role. She was fully occupied at home with the upkeep of the house and children: seeing that the family was fed, that clothes were washed and that we attended school as well as performed our daily chores. But most of all, she made sure that, as children, we would grow up aware of the family values, those things that held three or more generations together. They were values handed down from generation to generation verbally and played out in the daily lives of our parents and grandparents.

In the Caribbean, there is no Spring, Summer, Autumn or Winter. There is simply the dry and wet season. It was always father's eagerness to get planting that signalled the approach of the rainy season. *"I am going into the plot by the river next week because I want to start planting those cane cuttings before the rains. After that, I will put in the yams, eddoes, cassava and potatoes and then the green peas around the hedgerows,"* he would say. It was also the thinking of other small farmers. But my father was also a land-banker for, wherever there was a plot of land for sale within easy reach of the village, he would be one of the first to put in an offer. Apart from seeing it as an investment, he enjoyed spending much time outside his normal job looking after his crops. It was as though he had a natural bent for nature. He planted the crops but, except for the sugar cane, he left the harvesting and sale of produce to my mother. On any day during the week my mother would be summoned to the door by a hawker calling out, "Good morning Alice, what do you have for me today?" Soon she would be telling the hawker what crop was ripe and ready for sale and in what plot of land to find it. Hawkers - wholesale buyers - would arrive with very large trays, baskets or bags to buy bunches of bananas, bags of avocadoes, mangoes, breadfruit, green peas, okras and other produce to be sold in Bridgetown. "Get what you want and then we will cost it up," my mother would say and ask one of us to go with the hawker. It was a community built on trust.

Attached to the west side of the house and with access through the kitchen was a large brick oven. My mother was the pastry maker for the village and some of the surrounding ones as well. This kept her busy for part of the year but her busiest time was at Christmas when a kind of marathon baking would take place spreading over two days. Uncle Wilbert gathered the logs well in advance and allowed them to dry. He also fired up and stoked the oven, a task in which he took special pride. Once the cinders had reached the appropriate colour and grade for a given item, he would shout for that item. He knew the kind of heat required for poultry, pork, lamb, bread and cakes. Soon, with the sweat rolling down his face and the occasional wipe with a small towel taken from his pocket, he would carefully place each item on to the cinders using something that resembled a long-handled spade. Sometimes there would be up to twelve or more women over two days all carrying baskets of ingredients making their way to our house. I always enjoyed seeing my mother manage these activities: some women whisking eggs in buckets, others mixing the flour, sugar and grated coconut while yet others mixed the dough or greased the baking pans. My mother always cut the dough into appropriate pieces stopping occasionally to test that the eggs were whisked to the required consistency by others. Starting two days before Christmas Eve, the last person would often leave in the early hours of Christmas day. It was tiresome but my mother always enjoyed doing it, which is why we were not prepared for what was to happen on Christmas morning 1950.

On this occasion the last person left at about 3.30 in the morning carrying her basket of bread, pudding and baked pork. My mother, who had never missed a 5 o'clock Christmas Morning service at her local Brethren Church less than half of a mile away, decided she would go. With my little brother Frank and me in tow, she set out into a slightly chilly wind common in the Caribbean during the night at this time of the year. It was a gentle morning breeze impregnated with the sweet scent of morning glory, Jasmin, lady-of-the-night, lilies and the white elongated flower of ripe sugar cane. It all added to the spirit of Christmas but it was a feeling brought to an abrupt end that morning in church by the collapse of my mother who had to be taken home in an extended folding chair and put immediately to bed where she stayed for the next four days. Suddenly that Christmas feeling, generated by the sweet smell of flowers less than an hour before, had vanished. For us, there was no Christmas and no Christmas dinner. We were more concerned with her getting well. My father was able to put together something for us including generous helpings of ham, coconut bread and pudding, washed down with a soft aerated flavoured drink and coconut water. It was expensive to buy ham but it was the one meat every family would have on the dinner table at Christmas. For us, however, it lacked its usual taste for mother was not well.

Weddings in Barbados usually took place on Sundays so it was quite normal to see four or five young women leave our house on Saturday evening taking cakes to the place where the wedding reception would be held next day. Such miniature towers of white icing sparkled in the bright sunshine as the breeze ruffled colourful paper tassels suspended from the bottom tier. *"Make sure you don't trip,"* would often be her parting piece of advice as each girl left the house carrying a three tier cake precariously balanced in her hands. But apart from being a wife, a mother and the village pastry maker, my mother also doubled up as a village midwife. A knock at the window or door would often see her grab her instrument, usually a scissors and dash off into the night. Such was village life for my parents in rural Barbados up to and including the nineteen fifties. It was hard, it was tough and it was different to that I knew in Speightstown but it was one to which I had to adapt quite speedily.

14

Adapting To Village Life

Over time, I grew to know my grandmother better for at the end of every month our uncles, aunts and cousins would gather at our grandparents' house for a family meeting. It was an occasion to talk over anything bothering them, to share information and seek advice from each other but from grand-dad in particular. But there was also another reason for such a monthly gathering. With money contributed by all, grand-dad would buy food in bulk from Bridgetown every month: bags of flour, corn meal, sugar; a small drum of cooking oil and several other items which were distributed at the end of the family meeting. It also gave me an opportunity to meet many of my cousins and together we would spend the day playing in the nearby field or on an open pasture. Grandmother, with the help of two of my aunts, would be busy preparing a meal large enough to serve at least eight or ten adults and grandchildren. Two large metal pots would be going at the same time, positioned as they were on an open fire. It was a jolly time for us grandchildren but was also a way of my grandparents keeping the family of three generations together. Eventually my uncles and aunts and cousins would be on their way home carrying baskets of foodstuff. It was an occasion to which I always looked forward.

109

Dean Alleyne

It didn't take me long to adapt to village life for I was soon indulging in what boys of my age living in the countryside would normally do, like enjoying and sharing in the same jokes and even occasionally getting caught up in unexpected boyhood skirmishes. Most of all, it was with and through my little brother Frank that I would also have some unforgettable experiences. Tending the small flock of sheep was part of our daily routine especially on Saturdays since there was no school. It was in the afternoons when, after moving the sheep around to fresh grass and cooler spots or letting them have a drink in the tiny brook nearby, we would spend much time just running around on the pasture. We were free and felt free. To me it was a world touched by wonder, a world quite different to any I had ever known. There were times when, lying on our backs on the short grass beneath an almost cloudless blue sky, we would allow our imagination to wander. Frank would sometimes say, *"Looka dah little cloud Dennis,"* pointing to a small clump of clouds very high up. *"Wha it look like?"* After a few moments trying to establish which one he meant, I would respond by saying something like, *Oh yes, it looks like the head of a dog or even a horse, or something that was familiar to both of us.*

Such moments of silence, broken only by the chirping of birds flying pass, would find me taking a fleeting journey back to my days in Speightstown when Elliot and I would sit in a nearby field and just listen to the wind rustling through the tall grass. But nothing could replace the relaxed feeling of hearing sheep graze as they cut the short grass almost to the root with their teeth. It was the kind of tranquillity only momentarily broken by the occasional bleat of a mother calling her young lamb which would run to her skipping and jumping. Soon, with tail wagging, it would be enjoying a refreshing drink from its mother. Sometimes too, we would visit uncle John who lived very near to the pasture. There we would often get a piece of home-made bread and a drink.

At other times simply the sound of a car horn in the far distance would capture our attention high up as we were. It usually meant looking across the valley to see what car it was and where it was going for very few vehicles ever passed through the village since there was no through road. It was great fun to follow a vehicle with our eyes as it made its way through the village, commenting on the type, the colour and, if possible, the owner and driver. It was even more exciting if the vehicle happened to be a soft-drinks truck as they were usually painted in bright colours like the *Coca Cola* truck boldly displaying the brand on the side. Getting to St Simon's Village involved a steep climb for any motor vehicle. If such a vehicle was loaded, it would labour under the strain, but it was the whine of the engine that would trigger an argument between us as to what type and model could climb the hill fastest. From where we were high up on the slopes, we could also see most of the village below: the church all painted white with its pale blue roof, the school with its weathered pinkish walls, the old windmill and even our house. The whole setting resembled one from the Alpine scene in the film *Heidi.*

If it was the season for cashews or mangoes, we would spend some of the time wandering around, though not too far from the flock, in search of the juiciest fruit while talking about the simplest of things we came across. For example, a bird's nest would see us investigating what kind of bird and whether or not they were eggs in the nest, for the colour and spots on some eggs would often fascinate us. Soon, with evening approaching and with the blazing sun hanging low, we would untether the sheep and make our way home. It was always a wonderful end to the day.

Mango-scrumping was another pleasant pastime of ours even though we all had parents who had mango trees. It seemed as though the grass was always greener on the other side for it gave us a buzz to go after other people's ripe fruit. Like bees in search of nectar it must have been the bright red and yellow colour of the ripe fruit that attracted us. Whether it was daring or simply peer-group dynamics, we enjoyed it. On one occasion the moon had not yet risen above the nearby hills so it was still dark enough for us to get up to our usual mischief. We were with three of our friends sitting on the village church step, a forbidden area by the vicar but a favourite meeting place for boys and young men of all ages in the village to chat and share jokes at night particularly on moon-lit nights, a kind of local forum. There was a brief silence only broken when George had a brain wave. *"Dum is some ripe mangoes on old Martha's tree round de corner,"* he declared sounding half excited.

"So what," snapped Kelvin.

"Well, why don't we get some a dum," replied George with a soft grin.

"But it dark, how you gun know dah ripe ones?" asked Colin looking somewhat surprised to hear George talking about going after mangoes on a dark night.

"I know cause I saw dum yesterday and I was watching dum fah some time," he replied. This brought quiet approval from the rest of the group.

"Okay," said Colin, *"but how we gunna get at dum, cause de tree is hanging right over she galvanized roof?"*

"Yeah, wha would happen if a mango or two land on the roof?" said Frank laughing for, like the rest of us, he was already seeing the funny side of things.

"Well, we would all haffa run hard as hell," uttered George with the broadest of grins bringing a quiet round of laughter.

That settled, we set out to take the short walk to the tree supposedly laden with yellow fruit George had seen earlier, taking care not to let anyone see us even though it was quite dark. Looking around to make sure the course was clear, we made a sudden dash pass the galvanized paling and up the tree like cats in the night and were soon settled in convenient places where branches joined the trunk. From here, we could see the oil lamps in some of the nearby houses including, of course, old Martha's. In the dark, we used the technique of squeezing the mango to see if it was ready for eating. This proved to be successful as long as the stones were carefully released to the ground. Nothing was said or heard except the muffled hiss as we enjoyed ourselves with the sweet succulent fruit. Suddenly there was a croaking noise like that of a chicken as though it was in pain. There was a sudden hush, absolute silence prevailed while we tried to pierce the darkness with our eyes and pieces of mango stuck in our mouths.

"Wha dat?" snapped George in a hushed voice just audible to us.

"It is a chicken. I'll bet you some idiot squeezed de chicken head for a mango," groaned Colin with a slightly audible chuckle which triggered quiet laughter among the rest of the group.

"Who is de idiot?" piped up Frank, but before he could get an answer, the unfortunate bird gave out a screech so loud as to wake up all the other chickens roosting in the tree causing old Martha and the neighbours to push their heads through windows to see what was happening. George had seen the ripe mangoes during the day but he, like the rest of us, was

unaware that Martha's chickens roosted in the tree at night. There was nothing left to do but to take a dive. It was a question of everyman for himself. We were at various heights in the tree, some as high as four metres. To make matters worse, in his dive to escape, Colin landed squarely on the galvanized roof with a bang that brought some of Martha's family pictures crashing to the floor and triggering her into immediate action. She made a desperate effort to get outside and seize or catch sight of one of the villains. Her words matched the loud screeching of the chickens which by now had flown in all directions to escape us the intruders as well as Martha's battle cry.

Old Martha now had the moon in her favour for it was beginning to peek slowly above the hills throwing its first beams on the village and to reveal the wretched young lads. It was pandemonium. With the kind of rapidity only seen when a gun is fired near a flock of pigeons, we dropped from the tree each with thuds heavy enough to shake the wooden house. We took off in all directions through neighbouring gardens and small fields of cane, even scaling palings in the mad dash. Any mangoes stored in our pockets were soon jettisoned as we skipped or fell over uneven ground in our flight. To allow Martha or any of the neighbours to catch a glimpse of any of us would have meant a thrashing from our parents the moment they were told. We met next day and compared bruises we had sustained as well as the damage done to our clothes, bits of which were later seen hanging on prickly bush. Needless to say, it became the centre of amusement as we each tried to describe what happened and who it was that alarmed the chickens and how we each reached home. Every time we passed by old Martha's house, we couldn't help but gaze at `the scene of the crime'.

The Easter holidays had arrived and crop time was still in full swing. Sugar cane was already harvested from most of the

Walking Through The Pain

fields around the village allowing a panoramic view far into the distance around. It was about mid-morning that day when Adrian, George and John came strolling down the road. Adrian and John were both slightly taller than me and always on the lookout for a joke. George was short for his age but made up for this in his courage. The one thing we all had in common was that our short trousers were usually torn and our shirts would be hanging out. It was obvious they wanted Frank and me to join them which we did and we were soon sitting in one of our usual places, under a breadfruit tree talking about any and everything when John suddenly got up and brushed the sand from his backside.

"Leh we ga fishing fah crayfish or find some ripe cashews, fellows." We all looked at him and then at each other.

"Go whey?" asked Adrian, shooting an eager glance at him for he was always ready for any adventure.

"Wha bout de dry hill over the river in the gully?" piped up George, expecting a quick agreement. *"dum is lots of cashew trees over there and I sure by now deh loaded with ripe cashews."*

"Bring long a bat and a ball," added Adrian, *"we might be able to have a game on the riverbank, you know, not far from where de big rock overhangs the river."* We seldom left home without our game kit: a bat and a ball. After sharing two large pieces of coconut bread among ourselves, we were soon making our way down one side of the valley along a narrow tract between cuscus grass about three feet tall. It was a grass planted to demarcate one field from another but which sometimes could be taller than the canes. The natural positioning of flat rocks provided a kind of ford allowing us to cross the small stream to reach the hills on the other side. I was now very good at this for I had learned the skill from our small flock of sheep when taking them to and from

115

the pastures. George was right. There were lots of trees and ripe cashews too, some red, some yellow. Our eyes popped with excitement on seeing such an abundance of fruit. We were soon darting from branch to branch in search of our favourite.

"Who tell you these were here George?" asked Frank,

"I came here last week with my dad. *He said deh would be ripe this week,"* he replied as we sat in the shade of a tree feasting on the treat we had gathered and enjoying the scenery while cracking jokes on each other.

"Well at least this is better than jumping from Martha's mango tree in de dark," declared Adrian.

"But, I wonder who it was that grabbed de chicken head," asked Frank hopefully, gazing at John who finally owned up with a broad grin. There was a sudden silence. Something was brewing. As though telepathic, we moved together toward John, grabbed him by his hands and feet, dragged him down the grassy slope and hurled him clothes and all into the stream. We thought it a fitting punishment for what he had done to cut short our time in Martha's mango tree. There was also time to gather dried cashew kernels that had dropped from trees. These we would roast on an open fire later. From here, the grassy slope dipped down to the small stream which snaked its way slowly pass small plots of sugar cane, clumps of banana trees, cassava and sweet potatoes, all separated by hedgerows of green-pea trees. Overhead, the blue sky was occasionally broken by a white wispy cirrus cloud hurrying over the hilltop. In the near distance and to our right a small flock of blackbirds, attracted by the colour of ripe mangoes, were twittering away while having a feast. Having had our fill of cashews and a good laugh in the tall grass, it was now time to move on to something else.

We moved slowly down the slope toward the riverbank where there was enough of a flat area to allow a game of cricket to be played. The fact that it would mean one of us occasionally retrieving the ball from the river did not deter us for we had done this many times before. The bat was cut from the thick end of a dried branch of a nearby coconut tree. More often than not the ball was carved from a piece of wood and rounded with a sharp knife. Needless to say, you knew if you had missed the ball while batting, for the wooden object would connect to your shin with such an impact as to bring you plunging to the ground in agony sometimes with a slight bruise. With three pieces of the straightest branches we could find to be the wicket, the game commenced. But meandering around in the hills in search of cashews and playing cricket in temperatures of more than 30 degrees centigrade often made us hungry, which is why George always travelled with a box of matches in readiness to light up and roast, be it breadfruit, sweet potato, cassava, crayfish or even just dried cashew nuts.

That day we decided to go fishing for our lunch. We were soon naked and wading knee-deep in the shallow stream in search of crayfish usually found close to the river bank where tall grass or water reed cast a shadow over submerged flat rock. It was the dry season and the lack of rain meant the river was very low making it easier for us to see and catch crayfish. It took a certain skill to do this because crayfish, when cornered, tend to fight back by nipping you on the fingers with their sharp claws but Adrian and John were very good at it and had done a good job putting together a fair catch. Frank picked a ripe breadfruit from father's tree nearby and, with a small bundle of firewood gathered from around us, we were soon enjoying roast crayfish and breadfruit on the river bank. It was also an opportunity to roast the cashew nuts which all added to our river bank lunch. It was a perfect meal for five little boys who had nothing more

Dean Alleyne

to do than go around together enjoying themselves and whose parents were confident they knew how to survive. We were simply putting into practice some of the skills handed down to us by our older brothers and their friends.

15

Under Attack By A Swarm Of Bees

"Shusssh, you hear something?" snapped Colin turning his head swiftly upstream with eyes popping and ears as alert as those of a dog disturbed during its night-watch. "Something like what?" asked John, pausing for a moment halfway through a piece of roast potato. A dead hush quickly settled on the group so eager were we to hear what George had so anxiously drawn to our attention, nor did the noise of the nearby stream cascading over small boulders help.

"Yes, I hear a buzzing, like bees," said Frank looking up river from where he thought the sound was coming. With pieces of fish or breadfruit hanging from our mouths, we all looked up stream. It was in the direction of the massive rock which stood about fifteen feet high and protruded over the deepest part of the stream. We knew this rock well for we had often passed by it on our meanderings or had gone there to gather sagebrush which was used by our parents to ward off mosquitoes that tended to spring into action at dusk. The rock was also a favourite haunt for untethered goats which could often be seen at the top feeding on the tender shoots of brush wood.

119

Dean Alleyne

Today was different, for buzzing around a small hollow high up over the river, was a swarm of honey bees, their mottled bodies glistening in the afternoon sunshine. Although we all had seen a swarm in flight before, none of us had ever come so close to a hive. We knew bees could be vicious but sheer curiosity was driving us on to investigate with a view to plundering the hive. *"Leh we go and see,"* suggested John who, like the rest of us, was already thinking how nice it would be to sink his teeth into a piece of honeycomb with lots of golden honey oozing out. Leaving part of our roasted lunch behind, off we trotted a short way up stream to investigate. All sorts of thoughts bounced around in my mind as we approached cautiously. To begin with, the hive was at the highest point in the rock and at the deepest end of the river. It was as though these bees had deliberately settled in that spot to make it difficult for anyone to reach them. We decided to sit around for a while to see if they would settle down for we dared not go too close to arouse them. In the mean time we had decided that the honey must be ripe for cutting and that we ought to have a go, but the question still to be answered was who would be the one to get the honey comb out.

"Don't look at me boys, I know nothing bout bees or cutting honey," I said keeping an eye on the hive as it was known for a swarm to leave the hive and attack any seeming intruder.

"George, you should know bout cutting honey cause your brother Harold is good at it," declared Adrian.

"Yes, I used to ga wid he sometimes. He would first mek them drunk wid a smoking rag," exclaimed George. *"But how I going to get up there to the hive? Look whey it is, over the deep end of the river. I can't climb up there,"* he added, his face slightly screwed up as he looked at us for answers. We all looked up at the hive and then gazed at each other with a kind of contemplative look.

120

"I know, if we had a rope we could lower George down from above," suggested Frank with a wise look.

"Dah is a good idea but whey we going get rope from?" cried Adrian. Oswald who was the least talkative of the group sunk his teeth into his last crayfish before declaring,

"We can always get a rope from one ah dem sheep tied over there in that field." John glared at him.

"You always talking nonsense," he snapped. *"How we could do that and lef de animal to go astray? Just shut up and eat yah fish."*

"I used to see my dad cut roots from somewhere in deh other rock over there to tie things wid. Why we don't try that? We can twist them together to mek a rope," suggested Frank. The suggestion found favour with the rest of us.

Discussion over, we all moved toward the rock to gather some of the long hanging roots from a bearded fig tree.

"Did you know that the name Barbados comes from this tree?" I exclaimed, drawing from what my grand-dad had told me when I first saw a one in the village.

"How da ya know dat?" shouted John. They looked at me in bewilderment, even my brother Frank.

"My grand-dad told me that when the Portuguese sighted the island in 1536 on their way to Brazil they called it Los Barbados, the Bearded Ones, from the large number of such trees that were on the island." They all gazed at me in wonderment and then at each other. The tree can still be found in gullies across

Barbados. We were soon twisting a collection of roots together to make a rope long enough and strong enough to hold George from the top. This is where Oswald's knife came in handy for cutting the roots into suitable lengths.

The plan was for two of us to stand on the top of the rock and lower him with a smoking rag down to the hive to gather the honeycomb. We also decided to let him have some of our clothes to provide extra protection should the bees attack, although we felt that, with the smoking rag, he would be okay or so we thought. What we did not know was how tenacious and vicious in their attack honeybees could be when disturbed. With the rope now securely tied around his waist and a smoking rag in his hand, George was slowly lowered by John and Adrian from the top of the rock. Reaching the hole, he applied the smoking rag which seemed to drunken some of the bees inside causing them to fly around aimlessly, but others returning to the hive and seeing the intruder, were immediately roused to anger and moved swiftly into action. Instead of going into the hive they attacked anything in their path with relentless ferocity, including George who found himself in the direct line of fire.

"Dem up ma trousers and sleeves…help! help! pull me up, pull me up!" he shouted with screams that reverberated throughout the surrounding hills. With dangling hands and feet, he was the perfect target on which the bees could release their venom. By now they had found their way through any opening to sink their stings deeply into his flesh. To make matters worse John and Adrian who were supposed to pull him up were forced to abandon their post and head for cover in a nearby cane field as they too were viciously attacked by a splinter group that was not too drunk from the smoke. This saw the screaming George, in sheer agony and desperation, plunging helplessly fifteen feet to the river swiftly followed by a smoking torch and a swarm of

ferocious creatures in quick pursuit. His mind buzzed with quick flashes of thought as he hit the water with an almighty splash: *"perhaps if I stay under water* for *a while, they'll go away,"* but he had underestimated the tenacity of militant bees for, every time he surfaced for air, he was reminded in no uncertain terms that they were still there. Every time he raised his head, he was severely harpooned by these angry apian dive-bombers determined to get their pound of flesh. They seemed to have worked out George's tactics for, in his desperate effort to escape this onslaught, he made a mad dash for the canes only to be followed hard on his heels by this more than two thousand strong army of ferocious creatures. Relief only came when the swarm, probably having had enough of him, diverted their attention back to the hive no doubt to protect the queen bee, leaving George reeling in agony from a skin that was now punctured several times and that resembled a battlefield.

Meanwhile Adrian and John who had taken flight to the canes also found themselves hunted by a small squad bent on sinking their stings as deeply as possible into the boys' partly exposed skin. It was only the quick thinking of Frank shouting to them to lie down and roll that gave them a chance of shaking off this determined onslaught. Although we too had suffered the odd sting, it was nothing compared with what our friends had sustained. With the battle over, we proceeded to dislodge as many stings as possible from each other's skin. There was no more time for roast breadfruit and crayfish Instead, we made our way home to nurse our war wounds. The next day we compared the density of little mounds of flesh on our skin brought on by this onslaught. Needless to say, this became another topic of great amusement among the other lads in the village. We never mustered the courage to undertake such an adventure again.

Moonlit nights were always special for it was on such nights that

Dean Alleyne

all the children in the village came out to play under a moon that shone from a clear sky. So bright was it that some folk would often open windows and let the light flood every corner of the house rather than use their oil lamps. In fact, it was often said that you could easily find a needle on the ground. Villagers at that time did not have the benefit of electricity and street lights so the monthly arrival of the full moon was always something to which they looked forward. On such a night, grownups would be gathered in doorways or on steps chatting while children would either be sitting in small groups by the roadside telling stories or playing games.

16

Fun At The Seaside

*P*roximity to the sea meant we were always lured to the beach. It was soon after midday and the intense heat from the noonday sun had driven most villagers into a sluggish mood, something of a siesta. Old Ellis was sitting in the doorway of his house dozing, his head slipping slowly to his chest. Spot the dog sat panting quietly in the shade of a nearby banana tree. Cows in the nearby field were taking a break from their grazing to lie down and chew their cud. Even the breeze felt slightly warmer that day but we had other ideas. It was a day in the long hot summer holidays and, as we often did, we were sitting on the cooler, shaded east side of our house, the sun now becoming more intense on the west.

"*Leh we go to the beach fellows,*" shouted George, looking eagerly for approval.

"*Yeah, leh we go.*" added Adrian, sucking on a piece of sugar cane, excitement already showing in his face as he said so.

"*Okay, but leh me ask my mudda if we can go,*" piped up Frank. We could have cooled ourselves under one of the village stand-

125

pipes but doing so in the sea seemed more exciting. The ear-to-ear grin on Frank's face on his return suggested we had mother's approval.

"But leh we take long a dry coconut or two," suggested Oswald who made a dash home not too far away and returned with two dried coconuts and a knife with which to remove the white kernel from the hard shell. It was about a four-mile walk to the sea but it didn't matter as much of the journey was downhill and we had all the time in the world.

"Just a minute," I interjected, *"let me my bat and ball."*

"Yes, we might be able to get a game on the beach," blurted John. We were soon on our way pass the village church with its white walls and miniature bell tower below which was a set of ten steps, each about eight feet wide, leading down to the road from where the land dropped suddenly to form the head of a deep valley. It was on these steps that young men and boys gathered usually on moonlit nights to tell jokes and have fun until they were sometimes forced to dash for cover on the sudden appearance of the local vicar who resented such assemblies being held on church property.

Approaching us in the opposite direction was Mr James taking two cows to his house less than 200 yards from the church. Old James made a living by buying and selling livestock. He spent about two or three days going around the parish every week buying animals which he would then take to the market in Bridgetown. This he would do on foot so he was in the habit of giving them a good feed the day before he set out. As he passed we greeted him politely for to do otherwise would not have gone too well with our parents since you were expected to be polite to your elders. We were quickening our pace to give ourselves a

Walking Through The Pain

good distance between us and him when Frank began to laugh. *"Did you ever hear de joke about old James......?"* he asked, almost collapsing with laughter that was contagious for he had the kind of face which made you laugh even before he said anything. It is a characteristic of some of the best comedians. We gathered around him quickly to give him our undivided attention.

"One dark night old James was in de grave yard cutting grass for his animals." Here the grass always seemed to be more luscious than anywhere else.

"Well, wha den?" snapped Colin now very anxious to hear the full story.

"Well, on dis particular night de boys were on de church steps as usual telling ghost stories but din know that old James was cutting grass in the grave yard that night. The problem he had was getting out with a large bundle of grass on his head without de boys seeing him," continued Frank.

"Yes, but wha did he do next?" asked Oswald anxiously. This posed a major problem for old James for he would be in for a heavy fine by the vicar or the magistrate's court should he be caught. There was only one way out and that was through the very gate in front of which the boys were having fun telling ghost stories.

"He crept up slowly in de dark with the large bundle on his head and threw it over the gate into the group," continued Frank.

"Go on, go on, what happened next?" urged Oswald who always seemed to be slow on the uptake.

"Well, what would you do if you were in that group telling ghost stories on a dark night and someone decided to throw a bundle

of grass in the group at that time, you idiot?" Retorted Frank staring at Oswald in amazement. He then went on to describe how it sent shock waves and terror through the group causing the boys to take to speedy flight in all directions with fire flashing from their heels. In fact, one or two of them even ran pass their houses so scared were they. This left old James free to gather his bundle of cut grass and go home unseen. By the time he finished the story, they were falling about in fits of laughter.

We were almost out of the village when John called out, "*Look, leh we get some a dem plums over there on Sampson's tree to take wid we.*"

"*Over there where?*" asked George, his head turning this way and that way like a weather vane. "*I ain't see no plums.*"

"*Look, over there,*" replied John pointing to some ripe fruit high up in a tree about one hundred feet away.

"*Oh,*" said George, "*but we must be careful cause if Sampson catch we, we in real trouble. I know I would be in for a beating.*" We had to cross a patch of open land before reaching the tree surrounded at the base by a large clump of banana and plantain trees. After carefully surveying the scene, we decided it was too risky to climb the tree and that it would be better to try bringing down the ripe plums with small stones. With our pockets and hands full with stones we approached the tree like stalking panthers through a small patch of young cassava plants and into the banana and plantain patch to a convenient spot near the plum tree. From here we proceeded to hurl stones at the yellow fruit, dislodging five of the six ripe ones hanging high up. In our burning desire and persistence to get the last one, we did not see Sampson approaching quietly from behind with outstretched arms to grab one of us. The thud of the stones hitting the ground had obviously alerted him. The last ripe plum eventually fell to the ground. We all scrambled frantically to get it when Frank, the look-out man, suddenly shouted, "*Sampson, Sampson,*" triggering off panic and a sprint in all directions through a small banana grove and into a nearby cane field to escape.

We re-assembled about four hundred yards away to continue our stroll to the beach. We were approaching the last public stand-pipe in the village when there was a mad dash to quench our thirst. It was as though the swift getaway to escape the claws of Sampson and the sight of the stand-pipe had worked up a thirst strong enough to cause a hundred-yard dash to the tap, a very necessary pit-stop for the long haul through the blazing sun. Our thirst quenched, we continued our way down the hill each giving an account of the narrow escape and crossing the low bridge over the same river where we often fished, but this was not the time for fishing. Our sole intention now was to get to the sea. We were not far from the beach when George suggested that we stop for a while by Long Pond, one of the last remaining coastal wetlands of significance in the island and an area of outstanding beauty. This miniature lake receives water from a number of rivers in St Andrew before emptying itself into the Atlantic on the east coast. We sat in the shade of a tree not far away and allowed or minds to wander. Apart from the sea, it was the largest expanse of water I had ever seen.

"Wunna don't sometimes wonder whey all dis water come from?" groaned Adrian with an inquiring look through a slightly screwed-up face.

"Don't you know? It comes from all the rivers that flow from Hillaby, Chalky Mount, Turners Hall and all around. They all come together and flow into the pond," I exclaimed, drawing the attention of the group who gazed quietly at me in astonishment.

Dean Alleyne

"*Who told you dat?*" blurted John, taking a residual plum from his pocket and eating the flesh before tossing the seed into the lake.

"My grand-dad told me a lot about this whole area which he calls Scotland District because it looks like Scotland where his grandfather came from. He told me about the rivers and the valleys as well as Long Pond," I added, much to the amazement of my friends. This gave me a feeling of great satisfaction for I suddenly realised I was well ahead in most things, thanks to my grand-dad.

Such intense focus was only broken when Frank diverted our attention to the relics of the old railway bridge suggesting it was something worth exploring. We moved slowly to where rusted broken rails were protruding from both banks of a small river. They were the relics of the late 19th and early 20th century railway in the island.

"I wish the train was still running," I declared with a certain longing on my face.

"Why," asked George looking somewhat curious.

"Well, because my mother said you could get on it and go to Bridgetown. She said it stopped running before we were born but Elliot said our auntie Beatrice often brought him and a few of our cousins to Belleplaine to see it. He said that people from Bridgetown would come by train to Belleplaine on excursions but that it also carried sugar cane from Belleplaine to factories in St John and St Phillip," I added.

"*Yes, he is right because my dad sey it went from Bridgetown to Belleplaine,*" declared John. With the debate over, we continued on the last leg of our journey and within twenty minutes were rewarded with the sight of rising spray, the roar of Atlantic breakers and the smell of fresh sea air infused with the aroma of raw seaweed. Sand dunes like huge waves seemed to be rolling slowly inland except that, unlike Atlantic breakers with their white crests, these wore green crests made up of a combination of wild grape vines and other creeping plants which thrive by the sea. With hops, skips and jumps and with the sea-breeze in our faces, we hastened our way over the dunes ridding ourselves of our clothes on the way as we headed for the water. A series of yells indicated we had experienced a similar thing at the same time, namely, how chilly the water can be on the first splash even in the Caribbean. Having survived that initial shock, we were soon splashing around and bobbing up and down like corks on the ocean.

Overlooking the shore and rising sharply to a height of about one hundred and fifty feet are hills too void of fertile soil and blasted too much by on-shore winds to support any luscious vegetation. Except for the lower slopes which are covered with a mat of green creeping vine, these hills are mainly exposed brown sandstone and red clay, but are very picturesque. The sand dunes around us were buzzing with smaller children who, like bees in search of nectar at the base of flowers, were darting among the branches in search of tasty, dark red grapes or the meaty coco plum (known locally as *fat pork*) while their parents were either swimming around in the shallow waters of rock pools or enjoying bread, cakes and soft drinks from picnic baskets.

Approaching from the west along the beach were three lads about our age. It was clear that they would welcome playing a game of football with us because one of them carried a worn-out football under his arm. Brief introductions over, the game was on but after about thirty minutes kicking a ball around on the sand and taking several dives into the water to retrieve it, it was time to munch on pieces of coconut. Oswald proceeded to break the shells with a couple of stones and prize out the white thick kernel with his knife. We all commented on how nice coconut tasted when dipped in sea water. After having a good time, the two boys continued their way along the beach toward Bathsheba, a large fishing village further up the coast.

John, sitting not far away, was captured by the sound of small receding waves taking pieces of coconut shell and small oblong pebbles slowly down the beach. Adrian's attention was drawn to the speed with which baby crabs darted here and there over the wet sand. George found pleasure in throwing flat smooth oval pebbles out to sea, getting them to make two or three bounces as they skimmed across the water. I was focussed on the rock less than three hundred feet further east along the coast and less than fifty feet from the shore. It was about twenty-five feet high and had the shape of a large mushroom indicating the erosive power of incessant Atlantic breakers pounding away at its base and threatening to topple it. I looked around to find Adrian also gazing at the rock and at me with a mischievous grin.

"Evah jumped from that rock Dennis?" he asked with a daring chuckle.

"No," The way I held the word told him I wouldn't mind having a go. He stood up and brushed the sand from a piece of coconut he was about to eat.

"Hey fellows, why don't we try diving off dat rock over there? It's not too deep there and the tide is out now anyway." We took no more convincing.

"Cumma long," said George *"dah is good fun."* Waves breaking

132

on this rock sent spray over ten feet into the air while encircling the rock with white foam. Caught on the wrong side, one could be dashed mercilessly against the rock, but boys will be boys and we were no different at the age of nine and ten. We were dare devils.

"We could dive in and ride the waves going to shore," said Frank pointing to that part of the rock which was not covered with seaweed and therefore easier to climb. Very soon we were clambering up the rock like crabs and jumping on to white-crested waves rolling non-stop to the shore. From the beach, the picture presented was a set of black slender objects, living darts leaping from a large rock followed by a set of black heads bobbing up and down in a mass of moving white foam and using the waves to propel themselves to shore.

17

The Young Budding Entrepreneur

The sale of my toy car at the open day at St. Simon's School a year before triggered ideas in my head. Perhaps it was an expression of my early years with my adopted parents in Speightstown where I would see transactions taking place between my dad and other people. I did not know then that I was absorbing the significance of trading in everyday life. *"No one else in the village makes toy cars. Perhaps, if I could make more, I might be able to sell them like I did at the school open day."* It was an idea strongly supported by my mother. I set about collecting empting tins and hid them away from my brothers. I didn't want anyone to know what I was up to. I didn't know why, perhaps it was because I wanted to be first boy in the village to launch such a venture.

My mother was busy preparing the evening meal when, seeing it was a convenient moment, I asked quietly, "do you have an old pair of scissors, mum?" Busy as she was, she found time to pause and listen to me. I felt she knew I was up to something.

"No, but your aunt Beatrice is a dressmaker and she might have one but why do you want an old pair of scissors anyway Dennis?

What are you up to now?" she asked throwing me an inquisitive glance while rolling a dumpling for the pot. She could see my brain was working overtime and she knew I had the ability to look at an object and produce a good drawing of it and in many cases reproduce a good replica out of card or tin. She had not forgotten that it was my toy car that had attracted the attention of my teacher who had advised me to take it to the art and craft display on the school open-day and that it was there I made my first sale.

"I want to make more cars like the one I made for the school open-day and sell them but I need a scissors to cut the tin." I had her support and I was very excited for I was already beginning to picture boys in the village pulling my cars around, all made and sold by me. I was able to get a pair of old scissors from auntie as well as empty cotton thread reels to use as wheels. Soon, I was opening up empty tins and flattening them using a hammer and an anvil left under the house by an old friend of the family. Much of my spare time during that Xmas break was spent making cars that looked like the real thing especially when I added a coat of paint. Those painting houses were always glad to let me have a small portion of paint. Toy cars were in great demand around Christmas when parents were looking for toys for their children but could not afford those sold in Bridgetown. I did a brisk business during that Christmas season and beyond.

I soon observed that at different times in the year certain things were in demand. During the crop season, for example, boys enjoyed pulling empty flat containers around loaded with dried sugar cane peelings imitating trucks taking cane to the sugar factory. It was all part of the age of make-belief. *Why don't I make small trucks and sell them during the crop season. It only means getting small pieces of wood from empty boxes to add to the tin.* A picture was already unfolding in my mind of how I would go about shaping the driver's cab which I thought would be difficult. Soon the constant clanging of the hammer on tin during every spare moment told my mother I was up to something new. Occasionally I would look up to see her smiling at me busy under the mango tree in the yard, my outdoor workshop. If you could not buy a toy truck you could rent one for a few cents per week, but failing to pay the weekly rent would result in seizure of the vehicle. Not many boys allowed this to happen. The days when small boys in the village pulled empty sardine tins around pretending they were trucks had come to an end. Thanks to this one-man production line.

Easter brought a different demand. It was the time for kite-flying and every little boy and some grown-ups too wanted to have a kite. I learned how to design and make kites while on holiday in the Ivy District with my adopted mother by going to the house of a boy much older than me to buy a kite. Here I sat for some time watching how it was made. I observed closely how thin strips of wood were put together to make the frame and how different types of colour paper were added to give the kite a pattern and make it attractive in the air. I drew on what I had observed to make kites in the village. These I would leave hanging in the windows before leaving for school on mornings. My mother was happy looking after the sales. All this gave me a feeling of excitement and satisfaction on seeing my kites in the air over the village at Easter time. Success was already beginning to breed success.

With Christmas came another opportunity. In St. Simons and surrounding villages and indeed, in most of rural Barbados, it was customary to use a small branch from the Casuarina tree and decorate it to make a Christmas tree. As a small boy in Speightstown and the Ivy, I had noticed that Christmas trees in the show windows in stores were not made from casuarina branches and that they were decorated with lights. Indeed, I was accustomed to seeing one in my early years at home in Speightstown at Christmas, although how it was made did not matter to me at that time. However, on my visits to Bridgetown at Christmas while living with my adopted mother in the Ivy District, I had observed that fibre was twisted between two strands of soft wire to make it look like the branch of a tree. I wondered how I would get some of that fibre until I remembered bigger boys at the village school having to scrape leaves of sisal and bleach the fibre in the sun until it was white and then would use it to make rope and brushes. I soon realised that, by dying the white fibre green, I could produce something very close to what I had seen in shop windows in Bridgetown and like the one I had in Speightstown.

In rural Barbados at that time there was no electricity and hence no chance of having lights on a Christmas tree. My older brother Elliot was able to help me solve this problem by showing me how to connect four torch light batteries to torch light bulbs scattered throughout the tree. This I did after wrapping different types of transparent coloured paper around the bulbs to give the tree a more Christmas-like look. I was the first in the village and in the parish to come up with an illuminated Christmas tree much to the delight of my parents, my brothers and my friends although Calvin my eldest brother seemed to care very little about what I was doing. Encouragement came from all quarters except from him. In fact, he would sometimes say and do things to frustrate my progress. *What nonsense are you doing,* he would often exclaim. Any disagreement between my younger brother Frank and me would always find me in the wrong in his eyes. He never seemed to acknowledge my successes however small. It was something I could not understand. In spite of this, I pressed on and soon I was producing small trees about two feet tall. I now had the three main seasons covered: Christmas, Easter and crop time during which I was able to make enough pocket money to share with Frank my younger brother much to the delight of my parents.

There seemed no end to what I could do with my hands. My older brother Elliot was a keen cinema goer and liked collecting large black and white photos of his favourite movie stars. It was customary among many families at that time to have such photos hanging on walls in their houses. On one occasion Elliot bought two and hung them on the wall in our house. In his absence I removed one from the wall and looked at it closely to find that the photo was held in place with a tape and backing card behind a pane of glass. *"I'll try that,"* I said to myself, my brain again going into overdrive.

"Mother, can I try framing one of my drawings like those on the wall?"

"Yes Dennis, but which one are you thinking of framing because you did quite a few?" I would always ask her to take care of all drawings or paintings, many of which she often showed to my grand-dad or uncles when they visited.

"What about the one with the Sisal plant?" I suggested. She nodded in agreement. This watercolour had come about as a result of my fascination with the plume of yellow flowers at the top of the tall green central stem of a sisal hemp plant less than one hundred feet away from our house. It was a plume which was often host to a visiting yellow-breasted warbler all of which helped to capture my attention. It was an afternoon during the Easter break when I sat in the shade on the east of the house, the noon-day sun having moved sufficiently west to leave the east cool. It was from here that, with my water colours, I produced a painting of the plant for even at the age of ten I was gifted at drawing and painting using water colours.

I had misplaced the painting but with my mother's help I found it. Luck was on my side because I was able to get a suitable pane of glass from a window that was recently removed in the vicarage. With no means of getting the sticky tape used on the framed-photos my brother had bought, I cut a thin strip of paper and used watercolours to paint it in the appropriate colour. Getting hold of a piece of backing card was easy but, in the absence of glue, I used the sticky juice of a wild berry until I discovered that the melted dried sap from the mahogany tree did an excellent job. I hung my framed watercolour on a blank wall much to the delight of my parents and grand-dad who, on one of his weekly visits to see how I was getting on, remarked, "Alice, I always knew this little fellow was going to be good at art from very early. As a small child, he would come running to his dad and me showing us what he had drawn. It was usually a boat or something to do with the sea." As he said that, he tapped me on my head as he usual did only on this occasion, several times and with that encouraging look again.

This moment of delight and encouragement was suddenly interrupted by a knock at the door. It was the travelling salesman collecting his weekly payment for goods purchased, usually cloth. "Afternoon Alice, how are you today?" uttered Mr Rampasad with the smile of a successful salesman. He was always smartly dressed which was significant because in his suitcase would be various types of fabric for men's suits. He was very much liked by the villagers who depended on him for giving them the chance to buy now and pay later. It was one of the ways many families were able to clothe themselves. On entering the door, his eyes immediately fell on my framed water colour hanging on the wall.

Walking Through The Pain

"Who did this painting?" he asked as he enjoyed a cool drink of coconut water prepared by my mother, a welcome drink after his long walk through the mid-day sun. She looked at me with a soft smile as though to say *go on my son tell him who did it*. His eyes met mine. "Did you do this Dennis?" he asked levelling his eyes with mine.

"Yes, Mr Rampasad." I replied with excitement building up for someone outside the family had noticed my work and that someone was a salesman. He looked at the painting and then at me again with astonishment. He took the painting down and looked more closely at how it was framed and then turned to me with a look of satisfaction and expectation.

"If I brought pictures, glass already cut, card and the adhesive tape would you be able to do the same thing for me? I looked at my mother, my eyes popping with great expectations and I knew from her nod and smile what she wanted me to say.

"Yes, Mr Rampasad," I piped up smartly showing a keen interest and a desire to get started. I had just closed my first contract to supply a travelling salesman with framed pictures every two weeks. It was seasonal but it augmented my savings. However, on reaching the third year in secondary school, I had to reduce the time spent on such activities in order to apply more and more time to my school work but those years from ten to thirteen had seen me develop extra-curricular skills which brought immense pleasure to me and much delight and satisfaction to my parents. There was, however, one other skill that emerged purely by chance. My two older brothers and my father were the village barbers. Sunday mornings would see men, young and old, sitting patiently on stones on the west side of our house awaiting their turn. Needless to say, the wait although patient was far from

141

quiet for much of the time was spent talking about happenings in the village and making jokes at one another. As a small boy, I never joined in but I was always close enough to observe how my brothers did the job. My opportunity came one Saturday as my friends and I were cooling out under a coconut tree in our yard. It was George's untidy hair that drew Adrian's attention. Gazing at George with a slight look of wonderment he remarked with a giggle, "*George, you would do wid a haircut. You better not go to school wid ya head like dat on Monday because if you do, you'll be in for something from Mr Jones.*" Mr Jones was the head-teacher who, like other head-teachers, governed by the strap. "*He doesn't like boys coming to school with hair like dat,*" added Adrian. "*Why not let Dennis cut it fa ya? He must know something about cutting hair since his Dad and older brothers cut hair,*" interjected Oswald with the kind of smile that said he couldn't wait to see the outcome.

I had never cut anyone's hair before but I agreed because I was anxious to see if I could anyway. Since I was about to venture into the unknown, I thought it better to carry out this exercise with the greatest secrecy. George and I agreed to meet in a nearby field of canes in the late afternoon. Armed with a scissors and comb, I held George's head down in front of me in a kind of wrestler's hold and proceeded to carry out what turned out to be something just short of an execution. Almost every snip of the scissors brought blood from George's head accompanied by a muffled scream of agony, nor did I let up so determined was I to see it through. I had not yet learned the art of judging the depth of clip to suit the height of hair. At the end, George's head resembled a piece of land that was unevenly ploughed with scattered bald patches containing traces of blood indicating where I had lost control of the scissors. Unknown to us Oswald, Adrian and two others were hiding high up in a breadfruit tree not too far away and had a bird's eye view of the torture George was going through. As we emerged from the canes, we were greeted with an outburst of laughter from this group of boys so loud that it drew the attention of my older brothers. George thought it wise to stay away from school for a week to allow some of his hair to grow again. After that, I was only allowed to cut any one's hair in the presence of one of my brothers who would guide me through the stages. I was soon good enough to be left on my own and to make my own pocket money on Sunday mornings. In fact, I eventually got so good at it that I was the only one whom grand-dad would allow to cut his hair which was different and more difficult since it was straight.

18

Off To Secondary School

*I*t was at St Simon's Village School that I first discovered my childhood entrepreneurial skills but it was here too that I was given a baptism of fire on my very first day. However, in spite of such a traumatic introduction, I actually did very well in the two years I spent there, in fact so much so that I felt confident I would do well if I attended a secondary school. My adopted father had often made it clear that he wanted me to go to Harrison College and it was as though I had this burning desire to fulfil his wishes. What I didn't know then was that he had made the necessary financial provisions for me to have a secondary education and that my grand-dad was well aware of this. Perhaps, this was just as well since my biological father might have been less inclined to give me a secondary education.

He had become disillusioned because he was disappointed with Calvin, my eldest brother, whom he had sent to a private school but who had dropped out. In Barbados at that time children who had probably failed to reach the requirements for entry to a government secondary school or who had found it difficult at such a school, would opt to go to a private school which often did a very good job. Children in St Andrew had the choice of going

145

Dean Alleyne

either to the Alleyne Secondary School or to a private school not far away in the same area of Belleplaine. It was here that Calvin, when only in the second year, refused to accept the cane from his headmaster, choosing instead to engage in physical combat and his reluctance to go back to school in spite of my mother's efforts to get him to do so. According to Elliot, he would dress for school only to be chased by my mother on mornings through a nearby field to escape from her in hot pursuit. She regretfully eventually had to concede that he had no desire to return to school even after the head teacher visited our home to encourage him to do so.

The opportunity to satisfy the expectations of my parents and grandparents came on a trip with my mother to a parcel of land about one mile away to gather pigeon peas, a necessary ingredient to the Sunday meal. It was a Saturday morning when, with a small bag rolled and tucked under her arm, we set off to this plot of land about a thirty-minute walk away partly along the road and then along a very narrow winding path almost entirely overgrown with tall grass and most of it downhill. I was always fascinated by the greetings she gave and received from folk as we passed by their houses, some with shutters that opened upward supported by a short slender pole while others opened outward and were held in place by a long latch. *"Morning Alice, how are you today?"* To which she would often reply: *"I'm alright and how are you...?"* This would sometimes be followed with a little chat about this and that before we continued on our journey. The tract took us between small plots of canes hemmed in by cuscus grass so tall that sometimes I could hardly be seen as I trotted along behind her. This was alright until it rained for when it did, we would find ourselves walking along the same tract this time flooded by a temporary rivulet rushing down from the slopes above.

Just where the long slope levelled out into a kind of small floodplain stood a house of medium size. It was Sarah's, an old spinster who lived alone in what was known in Barbados as a four-hipped house: a house with the roof rising from the four sides of the building to meet in the centre. It was a very popular design in Barbados at that time. Sarah's was the only house on this small floodplain and, like most houses, stood on wooden posts high enough for livestock like sheep to be kept below. In her adjoining small plot of land, she grew avocadoes, limes, eddoes, potatoes and okras among other things which, together with the two breadfruit trees occupying central position on the plot, indicated that she was fairly self-sufficient. She was very short, in fact almost dwarf-like, though not the kind of person you could play around with for what she lacked in height she made up for in courage.

"Stay close to me Dennis, we have to be careful with those silly dogs Sarah has," advised my mother, but even before she could finish what she was saying, two brown dogs came rushing toward us barking profusely above us as we made our way along the sunken tract. Sarah never made any effort to call them off for it was as though she expected passers-by to defend themselves as best they could. I often thought these vicious creatures were even taller than Sarah herself. "You stick close to me," my mother said again, seeing that, as I was looking back at these frightening monsters, I kept stumbling over the occasional boulder in our path. To make matters worse, we were continuously sprayed in our faces with dewdrops which had settled on overhanging sugar cane and tall grass from the night before.

Even though we were now in a valley, it was not long before we began to feel the intense heat of the shining orb as it travelled slowly across the hilltops which seemed to lie close to its morning rays. The aroma rising from the floor of the valley was one associated with damp vegetation as it begins to heat. My attention was drawn to a small gathering of dragonflies (better known as 'pond flies' locally) hovering like helicopters over a nearby stagnant pond, their wings displaying a kaleidoscope of colour in the brilliant sunshine and were it not for the sound of a cutlass on grass breaking my focus, I would not have noticed old Tom not far away. He was cutting grass for his cow, a black and white heifer tethered to a tree nearby.

"How are you today Tom," shouted my mother, her fingers still moving swiftly from one branch to another. Tom was about average height and build with short grey hair. Even under the flat cap he was wearing you could see that the intense heat of the sun over the years had obviously taken its toll on his skin which looked dry and somewhat shrivelled. He was wearing a pair of dark dungaree trousers and sandals similar to those worn by my father and uncles. It turned out that he was a very good friend of the family for a long time and often dropped in to give my parents a helping-hand with any heavy work to be done around the house like helping uncle Wilbert with the oven. And, being a bachelor, he welcomed the occasional meal, a kind of *quid pro quo*.

"Hello Alice," he replied, raising his head momentarily to see and be seen, the sweat dripping from his forehead even though it was only mid-morning. He waved his hand and settled back to the job of cutting grass which sounded like our sheep grazing in the pasture. It was customary to see men cutting grass for their livestock and taking it tied in large bundles on their heads to where the animals were kept. Greetings exchanged, Tom got back to the job in hand and my mother to her peas. "Go and say hello to old Tom," she said with appealing eyes for she knew I had never seen him before. "Yes mother," I replied, carefully tucking a handful of peas into a large sack-like pocket tied around her

Walking Through The Pain

waist before making my way under a breadfruit tree and through a small potato patch to Tom whose plot of land was next to ours. I had never seen Tom before but he was willing to stop working and sit on a large stone to tell me something about himself, how long he knew my parents, his boyhood experiences and much more. I was always a good listener especially around older people so I enjoyed listening to his thrilling stories. Perhaps it was a characteristic I had caught from my adopted father who always listened patiently to what a person had to say before he spoke. There was no doubt that he knew more about me than I had thought.

"Want a coconut little fellow?" he asked, looking up at the tree just a few feet from where we were sitting. "Yes, thank you." He got up and took his knife from its sheath. I had seen this type of knife before for my uncles each carried one. It was a knife that appeared to be always kept very sharp for the blade glistened in the bright sunlight. Soon he was clambering up the tree to be followed within minutes by the thud of six coconuts hitting the ground in rapid succession. With three cuts on each nut he removed the top to expose the milky water. As we enjoyed the cooling juice, he took the opportunity to learn more about me. He was aware of my adoption but did not know how things had gone since the death of Sidney, my adopted dad. He removed a small towel from his pocket and mopped his brow.

"Do you miss Speightstown and all the good things you had especially your friends?" he asked, before returning his knife to its sheath. It was a question that triggered both happy and sad memories: *those happy times at the sea with my dad, playing with my friends, going for Sunday evening walks with Lilian but also those sad times when I realised I would never see my dad again.* An extended silence passed for the change in my expression told him I was reliving sad moments. He gave me a

149

Dean Alleyne

quiet hug. "Never mind little lad," he whispered.

"Yes", I replied now overwhelmed with such memories.

"Where did you live after leaving Speightstown," he asked as he got up to give his cow another bundle of freshly cut grass.

"I lived in the Ivy District. Do you know where it is?"

"Oh yes, it's in the parish of St Michael, a few miles out of Bridgetown and where did you go to school?

"I went to St Giles School. It……." Tom nodded his head and interjected before I could continue.

"I hear it is one of the best schools in St Michael. Did you like it and how did you get on?" he asked under a frowned forehead and a look that made me think he knew about the rough time at St Giles and the kind of life I had in the Ivy. He was now sitting again removing the white jelly from the interior of a coconut.

"I didn't like it but I did as best as I could." I refrained from telling him about my phobia for school and how it developed but by the end of our conversation, he had concluded that I would do well at a secondary school. He was a small peasant farmer but he was also aware of the benefits one could get by having a secondary education. It was what every parent in Barbados, no matter how poor, wanted for their children for it was seen as a way of breaking through that invisible glass ceiling as well as a family insurance for the future. Even at the tender age of ten, I realised what it meant to my family for me to have a good education. It was one of the driving forces that kept me on target even when things seemed to be going against me. Always fresh in my mind were the memories of the lifestyle I had in Speightstown as well as that enjoyed by our nearest neighbours and friends like the dentist, the priest and the two other shop keepers on Queen's Street. As young as I was, I was quick to realise that having a good education was my only way of returning to that life style.

"Here, take this coconut to your mother." I thanked him very much and returned to her carrying the coconut which she enjoyed, a welcome drink in such intense heat. After that, every time I went to the plot with my mother, I always looked for old Tom. I continued to help her pick the peas which had the kind of fragrance only freshly picked green pigeon peas have. Just then a flock of blackbirds flew over and settled in a tree laden with bright yellow juicy cashews, the very tree I was thinking of raiding before we left for home. By the time they flew off, having been disturbed by the loud mooing of Tom's cow, most of the fruit had been punctured several times revealing a yellow fleshy interior suggesting they were fully ripe.

We were sharing a couple of jokes, the kind that a mother would share with a son of ten when, after a brief pause, she looked at me with raised eyebrows. "Dennis, we are very proud of you and the way you are getting on at school as well as the prizes you get on 'open days' even though you had a horrible first day. We all know what you been through: losing your adopted dad whom you loved dearly and also seeing your mum lose everything and now attending your third elementary school and all this at such a tender age. However, we are proud to see that you still try to do your best." They had also seen how skilful I was with my hands and how thrifty I was with my ideas. Not only did her words boost my confidence, they also signalled that this was the opportunity to ask her a question that was on my mind for some time. It was at a time when going to a secondary school was not an automatic process. Instead, a lot depended on passing an entrance examination and then your parents having the resources to pay

Dean Alleyne

for your education. I put another handful of peas into her sac and gave her an appealing but determined look.

"Mother, I would like to go to the Alleyne School." The words were blunt but firm after which I shut up. It is located in Belleplaine, St Andrew and was built for twenty four boys as a seminary founded by Sir John Gay Alleyne in 1785 and upgraded to secondary status in 1875. My mother turned slowly and looked down at me with that motherly smile. There was an audible intake of breath. Perhaps in her mind were thoughts like: *I never thought I would live to see one of my children asking to go to the Alleyne school. I am glad it is you Dennis because your late adopted dad and Irene your unfortunate adopted mother would be happy. It is the kind of thing they always wanted for you and even though your father was disappointed with Calvin, I am going to see to it that you succeed.*

"You would son?" she replied, pausing for a moment to let her expression of delight hover over me. It was as though she had expected this request to come from me sooner. The air around us suddenly became impregnated with the smell of sage disturbed by two goats foraging on the large rock not far away. It was the very rock around which we had learnt a lesson in not what to do with honey bees. I had to restrain myself from telling her the story less she got annoyed with me but what gripped my attention at that very moment was the ability of these two goats to stand precariously on rocky crags and nibble away at succulent green shoots.

"Yes, mother," I replied still holding fast to my determined expression. By now Tom had cut enough grass for his cow and had decided to join us. He looked at me and then at my mother. "Alice, do you know that the Alleyne School is taking in new pupils next month?"

Walking Through The Pain

"No Tom." Her fingers came to a sudden stop as though frozen. She turned slowly and levelled her eyes with Tom's.

"Oh yes, and I understand that five or six children from St Simon's school will be taking the entrance exam. Is this little fellow one of them?" A blank expression spread quickly across my mother's face. It looked as though she was suddenly drained of blood for floating around in her mind were thoughts like: *my son is as bright as any another child in that school. How is it that no one told me about it?*

"No one told me about it Tom," she replied, the words trailing away for it brought back memories of how badly Elliot my older brother was treated when sent by the Vicar to join the staff as a young trainee teacher at the village school. Like most of the other members of staff, he had not attended a secondary school but had done exceptionally well as a boy at the same school thus attracting the attention of the priest who felt that he was quite capable and that with training, he could do the job. It was short-lived, five weeks to be precise. It was later discovered that my current teacher Mr Wilkie was the driving force behind the move to get rid of him. He had managed to persuade the head teacher to do so. Unknown to us, it was this very teacher Mr Wilkie who had quietly made arrangements for a group of boys and girls in my class to take the entrance exam in less than four weeks. It shocked my mother to the core on finding out that I was excluded from the group even though it was known I was quite capable. *"How could a child be given a prize for excellent work and then not be seen capable of taking an entrance exam,"* she pondered.

"That's a pity because I think this little fellow would do well at the Alleyne School," declared Tom as he continued to fill the sack with green peas.

153

Dean Alleyne

"Thank you Tom for letting me know." With her sack now full, we said bye to him and made our way home back along the narrow tract. My mother hardly spoke on her way back but there was no doubt in my mind that she was giving it serious thought. I felt hurt and disappointed. Quietly she went about the business of getting me registered as quickly as possible. On the morning of the exam, this little group of seven from the village school gathered at the teacher's house not too far away from ours to be taken down to the Alleyne School about four miles away.

"We will let them get well ahead because we don't want them to know that you will also be taking the exam," suggested my mother, peering into the distance to make sure they were on their way. Satisfied I was properly dressed and armed with ruler and pen, we set off and arrived about ten minutes after the group. Within a hundred yards from the school I could see the group of seven huddled together around our class-teacher in the veranda partly overgrown with a bougainvillea displaying its pink and red flowers in the crisp morning sunshine. I gazed at the group for a moment before turning to my mother with a frowned look for I was suddenly overcome with curiosity. "Mother, it looks as though you are the only parent here from my school." "Yes, I noticed that as well Dennis but never mind, you go in and do your best." It was clear to us that the group was looked after by our teacher. They were all surprised to see me turn up with my mother but none more so than the teacher himself whose face took a dive like a landslide.

By some means, he had managed to get everybody in the group to keep it away from me. I stood beside my mother away from the group. Within ten minutes we were all called in. Test completed, we made our way slowly up Haggatts Hill in the broiling noonday sun. She could see I was trying to work out why my teacher would do such a thing to me especially bearing in mind that I had gained a double promotion very soon after joining the school. I also kept thinking what would have happened if she did not get wind of what was going on. She tried to soften the blow by doing all she could to inspire me with every step we took on our way home. It was an experience that made me feel hard done-by even although I had passed the entrance exam. Nothing more was said about the saga until one day we were in another parcel of land this time gathering avocadoes when I turned to my mother with a rather puzzled look.

"Mother, you know Kelvin my best friend from up the road who sits next to me at school? He wasn't there for the exam either. Why? We were the two brightest in class four?"

"Perhaps Mr Willkie didn't tell his mother either Dennis," she replied. The look on her face told me she was hurt that Kelvin wasn't there and she could see that I was already missing my best friend. Kelvin and I not only sat on the same bench at primary school but we also sat together at Sunday school which we attended at the Brethren Church. In this small timber-framed church with its white walls, gathered my parents and grandparents together with other villagers on Sundays. Selected men among the congregation would be chosen to lead the Sunday service. Women were not allowed to play any part on such occasions. It was here too that my grand-dad played a leading role often delivering the sermon. I was always amazed by the extended moment of silence between each activity which was referred to as *'allowing the spirit to work.'* Perhaps it was the slightly muted sound of the wind stealing its way through fully opened windows that helped to create this moment of tranquillity.

At church the following Sunday, my mother learnt from Kelvin's mother that no one told her about the entrance exam and that she only got it from Kelvin when he came home looking rather depressed. It was the first day of the new term when he noticed that his best friend was not sitting next to him and was told that I had gone on to the Alleyne School. He looked horrified and shook his head when he was told by Mr Willkie himself. Both mothers concluded that Mr Willkie and the head-teacher didn't think their boys were of *the right class* to benefit from a secondary education.

"But why didn't he tell you about the entrance exam?" I was determined to get an answer.

"Son," she replied, "I don't know, but time is longer than twine. You must now try to do your very best at the Alleyne School. Learn well because we all want you to have a profession and we know you can do it." These words burnt indelibly on my mind. They were like jet fuel driving me through school. It was then that I knew what was expected of me and the part I had to play. Although all seven of us passed the entrance exam only three of us stood the course to take the final exam six years later. The others fell by the wayside. What is more, I was the best candidate for that year in terms of the number of subjects passed.

It was lunch-time on my first day at my new school and I had made a new friend, Julian. He was very short but made up for his lack of height through his academic ability and commitment to his school work. Indeed, he was the only one with whom I really had to compete for, although very good friends, we vied with each other seriously for that enviable position of first in the form at the end of term and the year. In fact, so keen was the competition between us third place always seemed light years behind. We were in a class of our own. The uniform for boys was khaki shorts and shirt but he looked even smarter in his scout uniform which was basically similar but with shoulder

Walking Through The Pain

straps and two pockets. When combined with the school red and yellow flashes over long socks, he looked well presented at all times.

We were strolling around the playing-field getting to know each other and expressing our excitement at being students of the Alleyne School. I had just retrieved a cricket ball from the hedge when I looked around to see in the distance a hand beckoning in our direction from the school veranda. It was accompanied with a shout: Dennis, Dennis. It was a student, a girl much older than me and like the others, Cathy was immaculately dressed in her blue and white uniform. Her pleasant smile enhanced with two large eyes and two plats supporting blue ribbons, suggested she knew me. We met halfway on the playing field. "You don't know me but I have heard quite a lot about you from your brother Elliot who speaks well of you." She adjusted my tie and I returned the smile. "I see you have made friends with Julian. That's nice, he lives not far from me and he is a clever boy," she added. Though we had joined the school in the same year she was much older and was three forms ahead of us.

Cathy felt it her duty to be my mentor. It was a role she performed very well, from making sure I was well turned-out every day to seeing I had done my homework and much more. The extent to which she confided in me was later shown when I became the messenger between her and her boyfriend at school. They could not be seen together and so it was a budding romance that had to be kept as quiet as possible while at school. During our frequent chats she always gave me the kind of confidence and inspiration a youngster needed to succeed. She was truly a kind of *in loco parentis* for me. It was a link only broken when Cathy passed the Oxford and Cambridge School exams and left for England to study nursing. She had played a significant part in my school career for she was a true mentor.

157

My first report at the end of the first term placed me third overall out of twelve. On the report were comments like: fair, fairly good, very fair and good for most subjects. I was elated with joy. My mother was thrilled and, after reading the report a couple of times, placed it safely on the dinner table for my father. After dinner, he donned a pair of fragile-looking spectacles he shared with mother and commenced to read the report with me in his presence. I shall never forget that day. Once finished, he called me to him, "I see you got a lot of *fairs* and *fairly this* and *fairly that*. I didn't know I had a son so fair," he uttered with a wry smile. With that, he gave me two tight ones on my backside with the palm of his hand. "Why 3rd? What about 1st or 2nd?" he asked. I was taken by surprise for I thought I had done well. The two smacks didn't hurt nor do I think they were intended to. They were merely symbolic but I got the message. I immediately knew what he was driving at *namely that I must do better than to come third for he was confident I could do better*. I was expected to do better than my best so, from the very start, I was not allowed to become complacent.

I did not disappoint him for, every year since that, I was either 1st or 2nd in the form as I went up through the school. I felt confident I could do it and I was determined to improve the socio-economic level of my family. So proud was my father that, as soon as I got home with my report at the end of the year, he would immediately take it around to his friends in the rum shop and around the village to show them how well I was doing. My parents did not have a secondary education but they had a fairly good idea of what it meant to have a good education. They knew I had the ability to do well and gave me maximum encouragement. As I progressed through school my achievements were backed by several prizes at each annual speech and prize-giving day. I can even recall receiving five in one year. It was this kind of

Walking Through The Pain

performance that contributed not only to my final results but to my eventually becoming head prefect of the school.

Speech and prize giving days also allowed me the opportunity of showing my parents how much I appreciated what they were doing for me. On my way back after receiving a prize, I would always pause for a brief moment and wave at them sitting in the audience with satisfaction and pride written all over their faces. It was my way of saying thanks. In the wing would always be Cathy waiting to smother me with congratulations. On one occasion, as the major entertainment for speech day, the school staged a few scenes from Shakespeare's *Julius Caesar* which saw me playing the part of Julius Caesar much to the delight of my parents. The strange thing was that the girl who played Metellus opposite me was slowly becoming my first teenage girlfriend for, as she knelt before me pleading for the repeal of her brother's banishment with the words: *Most high, most mighty and most puissant Caesar, Metellus Cimber throws before thy seat an humble heart-----Is there no voice more worthy than my own to sound more sweetly in great Caesar's ear for the repealing of my banished brother?* I was bowled over by her two large eyes under a pair of dark brown eye brows all set in a smile so beautiful as to melt the heart of even Caesar. I later learned that the teacher who did the role-casting knew that we were beginning to become attracted to each other. Father would always wear one of his best suits and being tall, he carried it off well. Mother was always neatly turned out with everything matching from hat to shoes. It was an occasion when they could be proud of their son and it was a delight for me to see them mingling with other parents.

19

A Denied Opportunity

The location of the Alleyne School allowed it to enjoy the cooling effect of sea-breezes bringing welcome relief to staff and students particularly during the afternoon. It was about mid-term that morning and the grounds-man had just finished preparing the cricket pitch for a match against the local cricket club that afternoon. The bougainvillea on the veranda was bowing its head under the intense heat of a noonday sun when the bell rang, indicating the end of lunch and the beginning of afternoon school. Within five minutes of returning to the classroom the headmaster arrived wearing a white jacket and carrying a small pile of books under his right arm. I was now at the school four years during which time I had become aware of how most boys perceived the headmaster. There was a notion among the lads that when he was wearing the white jacket someone would be in for a caning that day. Today was to be no exception and somehow, based on previous experience, I knew it would be a bad afternoon for me.

We rose to our feet as he entered and took his seat at his desk near the east window where he could maximise his intake of the cooling sea breeze. This was the rule whenever a master entered a classroom whether to take a lesson or just to have a word with a master taking a lesson. Failing to do so could bring wrath down on your head. He gave the form a piece of work to do while he called us individually to his desk to go through the French homework. It was my turn. I took up my position next to his desk. He had already made a number of red Xs on my book and, as I stood there, he made a comma with red ink large enough to cover half the page. "*I am in for it once again,*" I said to myself, my body shaking internally with fear. This was reinforced by that grim look followed by those dreadful words, *you report to my study after school lad*, words I had heard several times before and yet, every time I heard them, they struck fear in me. As I made my way back to my seat I could see the horrified look on the faces of the other students. They had seen it all before with almost seamless regularity. For the remainder of the afternoon, the thought of what was about to take place hung over me like a heavy sledgehammer about to fall on my head. This is not to say that others didn't have a similar experience from time to time, it was simply that mine occurred almost every week and sometimes twice per week.

I reported to his office for my weekly caning but as he raised his arm to deliver the first of three strokes on by backside with a bamboo cane, I stepped aside allowing the full force of the cane to land squarely on a box of chalk dispatching them to all corners of the room. I ended up getting four instead. It was as though this systematic frequent caning gave him a buzz, a ring-buzz I would say. It was a pattern observed by the other students who came to see such drama as a weekly event in which the head and I were the two players. But the whole experience eventually set me thinking. "*Was I that bad at French or did he develop a dislike of me?*" Whatever the answer, I was beginning to have enough of a situation that humiliated me more and more every time it occurred. I was in the first term of the final year and was now sufficiently pumped up to approach him.

It was after school one day when I knocked on the door of his study. "Come in," he said in a very forceful voice. "Oh, it is you Alleyne. What can I do for you?" raising his head to level his eyes with mine. I pulled myself to attention and without any preamble said, "Sir, I want to drop French." I had decided it was the only way to avoid weekly pain and humiliation even though it was the year for taking the final exam. I was not prepared to carry on experiencing such physical and mental pain at the hands of someone who seemed to revel in such action. Furthermore, by then he had killed any interest I had in the subject.

"Why?" he asked, the word popping from his lips like the fang of a rattlesnake and backed by that usual stern expression. I often thought that the reason for asking me *why* was to do with him losing his weekly expression of power and control. "I no longer want to take it in the final exam." This I said quite calmly but with a look of sheer determination. He sat back in his chair, tapped his pen twice on the desk and looked at me with his head at an angle. To my surprise, he agreed. Perhaps he saw me to be a lost cause in his subject anyway but, strange as it may seem, I succeeded in passing the subject using a correspondence course one year later.

But this abominable experience was followed within six months by another one even more bizarre. Up to the mid-seventies there were three front line secondary schools in Barbados: Harrison College (boys), Queen's College (girls) and Lodge School (boys). The major difference between these and other secondary schools at that time was that they offered subjects to Advanced and Scholarship Level. My grand-dad as well as my adopted parents always intended that I should go to Harrison College, so although I was attending the Alleyne School, my

Dean Alleyne

mind was always focused on Harrison College. It was deemed the crème de la crème of education in Barbados. My friend Julian with whom I vied for first place over four years was at the centre of my latest experience. We sat next to each other and were always seen together as he was my best friend at school. We discussed topics together and could often be seen or heard testing each other before a lesson. He was the kind of chap who would even cry if he didn't achieve first place. But it was a competition which was brought to an abrupt end in the fourth form.

The long summer break had arrived and I was paying Mr Vernon one of my usual Saturday mid-morning visits to take advantage of his pearls of wisdom. He lived less than two hundred yards away and taught at Belleplaine Boys school. We were sitting together on his front steps having our usual chat when he took a pebble and threw it into a nearby thicket disturbing a small flock of sparrows that took to the air.

"I hear you are doing well at the Alleyne School little Dennis, is that so?" The contented smile creeping across his face indicated he was very pleased to hear that, although not surprised.

"Yes." I replied with delight for I felt happy to know that he had received such news.

"But did you apply to take the scholarship exam for Harrison College?" He was expecting me to say 'yes' and was therefore very disappointed when he heard my response.

"What exam and what scholarship are you talking about Mr Vernon?" It was an answer delivered with a look of total surprise. It was a defining moment in our conversation and his eyes were instantly concerned.

Walking Through The Pain

"Do you know that if your friend Julian passes the secondary to first grade scholarship exam he will be going off to Harrison College for five years free?" Either I subconsciously ignored what he had said or I consciously couldn't believe it. The juice of a mango I was eating suddenly squirted from my mouth. There was a long silent moment before I levelled my eyes with his, willing it not to be true. Yet, I knew him well enough to know he would not make a joke like that on me.

"What did you say Mr Vernon?" the words leaving my lips with some difficulty behind a deeply surprised glare as I sat on the step looking decimated. He repeated the question only this time at a more even pace as he sensed it had not gone down well with me. He was serious. I was in a trance. *"Could this be true? How could this be? How could it happen unknown to me?"* were some of the many thoughts that bombarded my mind in split seconds. Though the school fee for Harrison College was five times greater than that for the Alleyne School, the advantages far outweighed the extra costs. Not only would I be going there on a scholarship but I would also have a chance to do subjects to Advanced Level as well as have a go at the Barbados Scholarship. I felt betrayed. It was now the summer break and therefore I had no chance of seeing Julian who, once he had passed the scholarship exam, would be starting at his new school at the beginning of the academic year in September.

"No, I didn't know anything about it," I croaked. What juice there was left in my mouth seemed to solidify.

"But were you not told about this kind of scholarship?" he said with a rather perplexed and disappointed look. "And didn't your friend Julian tell you about it?" he added.

"No" was the word that tumbled out of my mouth. Suddenly I

165

was stunned and distraught. For a second time in my school career I would be let down by the very person who, by his very profession, was *in loco parentis*. I could see a replay of the event that had taken place at the village school four years before. There I sat in speechless wonder.

"But you've always said he is your best friend and from what you told me he sits next to you at school." He paused for a moment, his expression revealing what was going on in his mind, thoughts like, *"What am I hearing? How could this happen?"* But I could also see that, contained within those thoughts, was a feeling of disbelief and sorrow that I had not been given a chance at the scholarship exam. It was the same Julian who sat next to me from the first form and with whom I keenly competed for first place at the end of each year. He was my best friend.

"So, you mean to tell me, nobody told you and your parents about it?" he continued looking horrified.

"No," I replied shaking my head in horror at what I was hearing, for once again I was denied an opportunity to move forward by the very person, the headmaster who knew I was quite capable. My tract record showed it.

"But didn't the headmaster announce at morning assembly that there was a scholarship exam coming up for those in the fourth form who wanted to go to Harrison College?"

"No," I replied, my body language rather than words saying it all for my answers were now monosyllabic.

"But that is what he was supposed to do, not just give one person the opportunity," he volunteered. "It was his duty to announce it at morning assembly and give those who were eligible

Walking Through The Pain

a chance. I am sure you have the ability to get one of those scholarships," he explained. As he spoke, I could see nothing but disappointment and disgust in his face. He knew it was unfair. He knew an injustice was done to me. That morning our usual discussion came to an abrupt end so hurt was I at hearing such news. In my mind I tried to make sense of it but over and over again came the same tantalizing question, *'How could my best friend Julian do this to me...a friend who sat next to me for four years?' Why didn't he tell me about it? How could the headmaster be so cruel!* As I made my way home I no longer seemed to notice the large golden apples hanging from the tree almost blocking my path, or even that my two friends Adrian and John from higher up the village were coming toward me. They beckoned at me but I did not see; they shouted but I could not hear, all of which was very much to their surprise. But what I did notice on reaching home was the look on my mother's face for, as she always did, she detected that something was causing me great distress. What was normally a five-minute walk home now seemed to be an hour.

"What's the matter Dennis?" She had seen that I had paid no attention to my two friends calling after me. I told her what I had just heard and she looked at me compassionately as we sat together for a quiet moment. I could also see that she was working out in her mind what she could do to ease my pain. She took a deep audible breath.

"I want you to go back to Mr Vaughan and ask him if we can have a ride with him if he is going to town today." She had quickly worked out that perhaps a day in the town would help to take things off my mind. On the way Mr Vaughan described the story to my mother and how he felt about it. My mother, who was no doubt thinking that here again someone was doing their best to frustrate my progress, remained calm.

167

Dean Alleyne

Mr Vaughan dropped us off in Tudor Street and, as the car drove away, she turned and with a warm look in her eyes, said,

"Son, can you remember I once told you that time is longer than twine?"

"Yes," I replied.

"Well, we got over obstacles before together and I am sure we will get over this one as well." I never saw my best friend again but such comforting words from my mother strengthened my resilience and galvanised my determination. The chair next to me at school was empty for the next eighteen months and even the other members in my class felt I was hard-done by. Yes, I had lost my best friend at school and yes, I was very disappointed and hurt but it all served to buttress my sense of direction and purpose. I went about preparing for the final exams with the kind of rigour, determination and grit I had seen in my adopted father in Speightstown. I redoubled my effort.

20

Tenacity Of Purpose

*D*uring this time, my parents and my brother Elliot gave me all the encouragement they could muster. Mother never allowed any friends to disrupt me when I was doing my homework. On occasions when they came to get me, she would say quietly, "Come here, let me show you where he is. You see that tree over yonder," pointing to a large tree about one hundred and forty yards away east of the house, "he is in it doing his homework." They always respected her wishes. The tree was a breadfruit tree in which I had a favourite spot just where a large branch joined the trunk. From here I could imbibe the view of surrounding low hills of brush wood and cashew trees, of rivulets hastening their way to form babbling brooks, and the small coconut grove with its resident flock of small monkeys. When combined with the gentle sway of the tree caused by light breezes, it provided the perfect environment for coming to grips with geography, history, or French and Latin verbs or just simply reading for leisure.

Apart from the occasional flock of birds flying above or the clang of a hoe or fork from someone working in the nearby plot of land, there was absolutely nothing to disturb me. Sometimes

Dean Alleyne

Mr Gilpin, an older member of the village, while working in his plot nearby would pause momentarily and raise his head on hearing me recite a piece of poetry. At other times I would see my mother peering at me from a window to make sure I was alright. Homework was also done at night with the help of an oil lamp. In the forefront of my mind was always a quote from Henry Longfellow: *And they, while their companions slept, were toiling upwards through the night.* It was with dogged determination that I pursued my goal. In the brief twilight my mother would make sure the transparent shade was clean and the wick trimmed for the night. Kneeling or sitting on a chair, I would press on with homework unmindful of my friends playing in the street. I would often rise at about five on mornings to complete any unfinished piece before having breakfast and setting out for school. No excuse was accepted for not finishing a piece of homework. The commitment I demonstrated was an expression of those values I had seen played out by my adopted and biological parents and grandparents. Those were the values that kept me driving forward at all costs. It was that burning desire to succeed that drove me to do whatever it took to keep working as hard as I could. I was determined not to allow anything, however frustrating, to get in my way. I was a young student on a mission.

But young as I was, I was quick to see an opportunity and seize it. I had already demonstrated this in my ability to see what was needed among children in the village and try to satisfy that need. Whether this was genetic or part of my early upbringing I don't know but it played a significant part in my life. This was further demonstrated shortly after my first year school report when I noticed two youngsters much older than me having private tuition from a teacher in the village. I had also seen his name displayed on the school awards board as having done very well in the Oxford & Cambridge exams and I was quick to realize that, even though I was making good progress, I could still benefit from additional help. Such an opportunity arose on one of my visits with my mother to one of her cousins. Jessica lived in a small village clinging to the north facing slopes of a ridge, one of the highest points in the island which, by its location and altitude, attracted some of the heaviest rainfall. This together with the heat encourages the growth of luscious vegetation including fruit trees so tall that they seem to be competing with each other for the sun: breadfruit, golden apple, mango, plantain, pawpaw, shaddock, avocado and much more.

Nestled in this luscious fruit grove sits Carrington's Village with a small group of timber-frame houses similar to those in other villages. In this setting where the land on the north side of the road fell sharply to a depth of ten feet, stood a small two-gabled wooden house which, like others on this side of the road, stood on a number of tall vertical posts sunk deeply into the ground. It was here that I enjoyed a glass of ginger beer and a tasty piece of cake for it was the home of cousin Jessica and her son Freddie, a young teacher, whom I grew to like and admire very much. The area also attracted early morning mist and you could still hear and feel the pitter-patter of rain drops from the overhead foliage long after the passing of a rain shower. I always knew when we were getting there because there seemed to be a change in the air which felt heavier due to the build-up of moisture.

It was a long arduous journey on foot of about eight miles most of which was uphill, but my mother would always take me with her rather than Frank. I was curious although I never asked why. We were about half way there on this occasion when we made a brief stop to have a piece of home-made bread and ginger beer. She slowly removed her hat and allowed the air to flow through her hair before turning to me with a half glance. "Dennis, don't you sometimes wonder why I always bring you along with me instead of Frank?"

Dean Alleyne

"Yes mother. Is it because I'm older and can keep up with you on the long walk?" I replied, expecting her to say yes. Instead, she smiled.

"Oh no, it's not that. I bring you along because I want you to take a page out of Freddie's book. I want you to see him as a good example. Don't you see how he talks to you and gives you ideas of what to do at school in order to do well?"

"Yes mother," I replied, nodding in quiet agreement, a few crumbles of bread escaping from my mouth as I did so. I now had my eyes fixed firmly on hers because I could see she had more to say.

"Well, I would like you to follow in his footsteps because he also went to the Alleyne School and, although he too lost his father when he was just a kid, he did very well indeed." I got the message loud and clear. With our hunger satisfied we were on our way. Freddie was Jessica's only child who had joined the teaching service after finishing school. He was much older than me but being a teacher he was able to relate to me and what I was doing at school. I always looked forward to visiting my relatives in Carrington's village. My mother was on the right tract for such visits spurred me on to see him as a role model especially as he would give me any second-hand text books he no longer needed. It was at a time when it was very difficult to get hold of new text books.

The whole experience of getting to know Freddie together with my mother's admonishment that day set me thinking. I had just arrived home from school and no one was at home but my mother busy preparing the evening meal. This gave us an opportunity to reflect on what a nice day we had on our last visit to cousin Jessica and how much I had learned from Freddie.

172

"Mother, can you take me on Saturdays to Freddie for private lessons?" She knew from the tone of my voice that I was serious. After adding two more dumplings to the soup boiling away on an open fire, she briskly wiped her hand with the short apron she was wearing before resting her hand on my shoulder.

"I would like to do so son but it is too far for us to do that journey every Saturday." As she spoke, I could sense she regretted not being able to fulfil my request which it seemed she had anticipated would come sooner or later. But I could also see she had already come up with an alternative. "But I'll tell you what I will do. I'm going to ask Mr Dottin if you can join his Saturday class."

Mr Dottin was a local teacher who taught at Hillaby Village School, the very village that was the end of the journey by bus on my return to St Simon. I had also seen his name engraved on the awards plaque at the Alleyne School. Her words were like music to my ears and in less than two weeks I had joined Mr Dottin's Saturday class. It was here that I had my Maths, English and Latin reinforced but it was here too that I had an another unforgettable but bizarre experience. We were doing a piece of English which required us to finish a number of common proverbs. For instance, *a stitch in time saves nine*. "Your turn Dennis," he said. "A bird in the hand ...." I stood up. I was in a naughty mood. I knew the answer and Mr Dottin knew I did, but instead of giving him what he expected, I thought I would be clever and make a joke on him. "*A bird in the hand is not as good as two in the stomach,*" I uttered with a wry smile. The correct answer should have been *a bird in the hand is worth two in the bush.*

I had hardly completed the answer when his eyes popped. He knew immediately what I was trying to do and reached for his cane. Without a moment to spare, I bolted through the nearest window and made two orbits of the house hotly pursued by him with a raised cane. Seeing he was catching up, I quickly decided to leave the orbit and shoot off home with sparks flashing from my heels. So close was he that I had to run pass my house and head for a field of canes. There I remained still until I knew he had given up the chase. I crept home later looking rather sullen. "What are you doing home? Why are you not at Mr Dottin?" asked my mother anxiously, but seeing I looked exhausted, gave me a glass of water from the monkey (that water jug for keeping water cool) in the window. I related the story between panting and sips of water. To my surprise she found it rather amusing but insisted that I go back and apologise. Of course, I never tried anything like that again for I learned that Mr Dottin took his job very seriously.

21

My Brother Comes To The Rescue

*I*t was mid-afternoon on a hot day in July near the end of term and the Alleyne School was playing a cricket match against the Coleridge & Parry School from St Pater. I had also received news that I had done well in the Oxford and Cambridge Schools Exams. On the visiting team was a boy who caught my immediate attention. *I think I know that fellow, he was with me at Speightstown primary school.* I stood gazing quietly when the captain called out, come on Dennis, we are ready to take the field. I turned and joined the others. He opened the batting for his school and did very well scoring his first fifty runs. He was therefore at the wicket long enough for me to convince myself that we were schoolboys together at Speightstown boys school and that he was one of us standing inside the school gate on our first day. During the interval, we made haste to reach each other for he had a similar thought. He was at first as puzzled as I was before he too concluded we were small boys together at the same primary school. In the fifteen minutes allowed, we were able to re-establish contact while tucking into a piece of cake and a glass of ginger beer. We chatted about exam results which were good all round.

175

Dean Alleyne

"Are you going to do the Advanced Levels next year?" he asked, his eyes beaming with delight and expectation.

"Unfortunately no," I replied with a shake of the head. I had considered the idea but had no knowledge of how to go about it.

"But why aren't you?" he asked looking very surprised under a furrowed forehead.

"You cannot do the Advanced Levels here at the Alleyne School." At least I knew that you needed graduate level teachers to take you to A-Level standard and that no one of the staff had a degree.

"Yes, but what about Harrison College? Have you tried getting into the sixth form there?" Even then as he said that, I could not quite get to grips with how it would take place.

"I don't know how to go about it," I replied looking very attentive.

"Don't you know that once your results are good you can get a transfer to Harrison College? I got one from Coleridge & Parry to Harrison College based on my results and I am starting next term. Why don't you ask the headmaster to do the same for you?" At this point he was summoned to take the field with his team but not before giving me a glimmer of hope. There was still a chance I could make it. Next day, I went to see the headmaster expecting his approval and assistance in the pursuit of my dream (I don't know why) namely, to attend Harrison College and acquire the Advanced Level in three subjects. I approached his office that afternoon to find the door slightly ajar. I knocked and was immediately invited in, perhaps it was one of the perks of being head boy. "Congratulations Dennis, you did well in your exams." Based on past experiences I found it difficult to work

176

out whether it was meant to be a compliment, a mere greeting or a sign of what was to come. I straightened myself up. A late afternoon breeze, floating across Long Pond, crept through the window ruffling some papers on his desk. "Sir, I would like to go to Harrison College to do the A-Levels." This I said without any preamble. He was sitting at his table as usual marking homework and it seemed as though he was bent on finishing the set of books before responding to my request. Eventually he looked up, pressed himself firmly against the back of his chair and stared at me with squinted eyes under a furrowed brow. It seemed as though he didn't expect such a request from me. I didn't know why. What I did know was that I had to be very careful because, apart from knowing what to expect when he wore his white jacket, he was very unpredictable. Just then I recalled him canning a head-boy on his last day at school merely because he caught him giving a girl a parting kiss on her cheek.

"What would you like to do?" The words came from a face that had suddenly gone chiselled confirming my worst fears. Straight away, I sensed it was not going to be easy trying to enlist his assistance. I inhaled as much of the fresh sea breeze coming through the window as possible and cleared my throat.

"I would like to go to Harrison College to take Advanced Level History, Latin and English, Sir," I repeated. This time he looked squarely at me less aggressively. He was preparing me for his next move.

"But you don't have to go to Harrison College to do the A-Levels, you can do them here and you could be the first to do so," he suggested, the words leaving his lips slowly. My mind boggled at the very idea. I started to chuckle inside. *"Here we go again,"* I said under my breath. *"What a load of nonsense. There is no one here qualified to teach any subject to A-Level standard."* What

Dean Alleyne

I did not know was that his response was a subtle reference to his non-interest in my desire to fulfil a personal aspiration. It was not long before the heated argument between us seemed to be driving up the mid-summer heat that afternoon forcing him to discard his white jacket and me to mop my brow. *Why do I expect him to help me after what he did only two years ago regarding the secondary to first grade scholarship exam?* I pondered.

"But sir, there is no one here to teach subjects up to A-Level standard," I said vehemently and with an expression that clearly suggested I disagreed totally. There were only four teachers at the school including the head and none had a degree. At least I knew that you needed to have a degree to teach to A-Level. Seeing that I was determined to stand my ground, he pulled another book from the pile and continued his marking. There was a short interval when nothing was said. It was an agonising silence only broken by the flapping of a shutter.

"Okay, I will contact the head of Harrison College and make the necessary arrangements for you to start in September, the beginning of the new academic year. Come and see me during the holidays and I will let you know what's happening." That said he hurriedly got back to his marking.

"Thank you, Sir." *Should I be pleased about this or am I whistling in the wind,* I thought to myself as I walked away slowly, I could feel his insincerity like a poisoned arrow piercing my skin. In spite of this, he was the headmaster and I was prepared to give him the benefit of the doubt. I was elated with joy knowing that may be, yes just may be, I would finally make it to Harrison College. I would soon be wearing a pair of grey trousers, a white shirt and that 6th form school tie while pursuing three A-Level subjects. I would at last be attending the school of my grand-dad's and

Walking Through The Pain

late adopted father's choice. My parents were delighted with the news although my mother's face assumed an expression indicating she did not feel reassured as long as the headmaster was involved. Such were her powers of perception.

During the long summer break, I visited the headmaster as he suggested. After three such visits I realised nothing had been done. Instead, I was always shunted of with an excuse why he was unable to do so. The new term had now started and, seeing nothing was done and the term was slipping away, I turned in sheer desperation to my older brother Elliot for help for by then it became quite clear to me that the head had no intention of carrying out his promise. As soon as he heard the story, he immediately made his way to the local police station and made a phone call that was to bring about a significant change in my life. The police station and the doctor's office were the only two places having a phone in those days. He called the headmaster of Harrison College, told him the story and secured an appointment to see him the following Sunday at 3pm at his residence.

My father rented a car and, with Elliot driving, we arrived at the headmaster's residence in Roebuck Street at the appointed time. He was from England, short and slightly burly with a balding head behind a pair of turtle shell framed glasses. I described the entire story and how much I was looking forward to joining the college. Sitting in his armchair, he gave two puffs on his pipe and placed it gently on a small table next to him without speaking for a drawn-out moment. As the smoke drifted through a nearby window he was able to discern my burning desire to join the school. He took up his pipe again and knocked it twice on the handle of his chair before dipping his head and popping his eyes over his glasses with a look of disappointment. "But I never heard from the head of the

179

Dean Alleyne

Alleyne School throughout the summer break. Had he got in touch with me you would have been here from the beginning of the academic year."

My worse fear had become a reality. My father and Elliot could see he was very disappointed that the head of a secondary school could do such a thing to a student who was not only anxious to achieve A-Level certificates but was qualified to follow the courses. On hearing such news, I was stunned though I don't know why based on his tract record with me. I could not believe that the headmaster would be so negligent. As though planned to mellow my boiling emotions, the maid entered carrying a tray of tea and cakes for four. She was short, a local girl but quite attractive. Her body language suggested it was unusual for the headmaster to interview on a Sunday afternoon and that it must have been something of great significance causing him to do so. After making sure we were all served with light refreshments she turned and, having adjusted a curtain at the window which was slightly dislodged by the breeze, left the room.

"We will get you registered to start next term in January. You will be joining the Modern Sixth to do Latin, English and History. Of course you will have some catching up to do. Come and see me again next week when I will be able to give you your set of text books and timetable." He handed my father a booklist with prices. We thanked him very much and started on our return journey home. As though anticipating the outcome, my mother in her humble way had prepared a special meal for the Sunday evening. We sat at the table, excitement pervading the entire house. No one before within the immediate family circle had had a secondary education. Now here I was, about to enter the corridors of the top and most prestigious school in the island. If I did not know before, it was then I realized quite a lot rested on my shoulders.

Walking Through The Pain

"You must study hard, my boy, like you did at the Alleyne School. We are all very proud of you. Sidney, your adopted dad would have been very pleased with how well you have done," declared my father with a confident look as he poured himself, mother and Elliot a shot of rum.

"We want you to be the brightest in the village. You get a good education and you can go anywhere and get a good job or a profession," piped up my mother while spooning rice and peas, pot-pork and gravy on to each person's plate. My brother Elliott was busy diving into his meal when he managed to raise his head and speak with an expression of sheer disgust giving way slowly to delight.

"I don't think the headmaster of the Alleyne School wanted you to go to Harrison College. He probably thinks it is too high for you. After all, why should a boy like you be given such an opportunity! Don't forget what he did to you just two years ago. He told you nothing about the scholarship exam. Perhaps, if he had done that, we wouldn't have to pay twenty-five dollars a term for you now. Never mind, don't worry about him. You just show him you can do it, little brother."

As he said that, my mother got up and lit the oil lamp in the corner because twilight was fast fading and mosquitoes were beginning to signal their entrance. Soon she brought us cups of hot chocolate to round off what was indeed a successful day. The next three weeks saw her busy getting together two pairs of grey trousers and white shirts for me. The school badge and tie had to be purchased from the school. Once again my brother took care of that. I was anxiously looking forward to the first day because, apart from anything else, it would also be my first go at wearing long trousers. My parents were seeing their son move into another phase of development.

181

Dean Alleyne

The bus from St Simons Village to Bridgetown ran on Mondays, Wednesdays, Fridays and Saturdays. There was only one morning departure at 7:30 but it was quite convenient for me since it arrived in Bridgetown in time for me to take a short walk along Broad Street to school. On Tuesdays and Thursdays, I would sometimes join two of my friends on a fifty-minute walk through Turners Hall Wood to an alternative bus just outside of Turners Hall Primary School near Hillaby Village. My first day was a Tuesday and, now dressed as a Harrisonian, I set out with my bag of books to join my two friends Errol and Neville from higher up the village who were already attending a private secondary school in town. As we made our way through the woods still slightly chilly from the night before, we chatted about the kind of things boys of sixteen tend to talk about. The journey was up hill all the way to the bus terminus, the very spot from where less than eight years ago I had my first glimpse of where I was about to live. From here I was able to look back on that dark mass which struck fear in me when I first saw it. Words could hardly express the joy I felt on the first day when I passed through those large wrought-iron gates with the letters HC. It was *'a dream come true'*. I had succeeded in doing so *against all odds*. What is more, I was placed in the same sixth form as my friend whom I had met that day on the cricket field at the Alleyne School. We did History, Latin and English to advanced level together.

Sometimes if it rained the night before, I would opt to do the walk to the outskirts of Belleplaine on a Tuesday or Thursday morning to take another bus from a pick-up point not far from Haggatts Sugar factory. To take the fifty-minute walk through the woods on a rainy morning would mean getting rained on from overhanging foliage long after the rain had stopped. Most mornings I would be fully equipped for school but just occasionally I would have neither the bus fare nor lunch money. On reaching Haggatts factory on way to the pick-up point, I would seek help from my brother who worked as a young engineer. He always seemed to know what I wanted even before I could tell him because, as I approached him, he would be delving into his pocket to find me the necessary funds for the day. There were times when he actually emptied his pocket to satisfy my immediate needs for he was always glad to help his little brother.

22

Boys Will Be Boys

Almost encircling the village of St Simon's was Cheltenham, a thirty-acre Plantation under sugar cane and once owned by a great-great uncle of mine. At one time, it provided much work for some of the local villagers in planting and caring for the crop but also for those who worked at the windmill and in the boiler house to produce syrup. Now disused, the millhouse became a gathering spot for three youngsters: Claude, the son of the current owner, Lester, the last son of the head-teacher of the village school and me. We were all at different secondary schools but being roughly of a similar age we always found time to meet in the millhouse particularly during the long, hot summer holidays to chat about what was happening at school or just go for long walks. The demise of windmills meant that small sugar cane plantations sent their cane to one of the nearest sugar factories. Claude's dad sent his to Haggatts or Bruce Vale, two of the three sugar factories in St Andrew at that time.

Claude's dad had a truck he used for this purpose but, like other plantation owners, he also had a car on which Claude, with the aid of one of his dad's drivers, would learn to drive in the large

Dean Alleyne

court yard between the boiler house and the mill during his dad's absence. In fact, he eventually become sufficiently good for his dad to allow him to run short errands with the car just outside the village but he was never allowed to go long distances. The crop season had come to an end and, as usual, we were chilling out in the old millhouse opening the shells of dried almonds which had fallen from the tree in the yard when Claude suddenly blurted out with a broad smile, "Come on fellows, let's go for a drive somewhere." He was also a daring chap and there was no knowing what he would do next. Lester and I concluded that, because he was not very good at school, he was always ready to do other things to compensate. We looked at each other again quickly before throwing our gaze at Claude. "Yes, why not," piped up Lester. We needed no more convincing. The disused boiler house had been converted to a shop in which Claude's mother was busy serving customers and therefore was completely unaware that the three of us had quietly taken the car.

His dad would often leave the car parked under an almond tree near the boiler house if he was using the lorry. Dressed in short khaki trousers, short-sleeved shirts with tails hanging out as usual and barefooted, we piled into the Vanguard, a late 1950's car. As we did so I wondered what would happen if his dad got back home before us, but it was something different and exciting to do. As we set off slowly through the village, Lester and I took the opportunity to wave at some of the other boys who seemed puzzled at seeing three youngsters like themselves going somewhere in a car on their own. We were passing Haggatts factory when Claude suddenly shouted out, "Where shall we go boys? It can't be too far because I must get back before daddy returns with the truck." "Let's go by our friends in Airy Cot," volunteered Lester to which there was an immediate consensus. Airy Cot was a small village resting on a hilltop about five miles away. From here, the land drops away steeply to form gullies

186

so deep in places as to make farming difficult if not impossible. The village was much smaller than St Simon's but it had its own primary school of ninety pupils and headed by the father of our two school friends whose sisters also attended secondary schools in Bridgetown and who often travelled on the same school bus as us. After having fun over soft drinks, sandwiches and cake provided by their mother, we headed for home elated with joy and chatting about what a pleasant afternoon we had but we were not prepared for what was soon to follow.

Next year's crop of cane was already tall and overhanging the road in some places making it a bit difficult to have a clear view ahead. We were on a fairly narrow stretch of road chatting about this and that when we suddenly came to a bend where the canes were almost a quarter of the way over the road, forcing Claude to veer off his side to avoid the car being battered by overhanging cane. We were thoroughly enjoying ourselves when Lester quickly jumped up from his seat banging his head against the roof of the car in the process. "Look out," he shouted at the top of his voice. My eyes popped at seeing this fast approaching mass of danger. We did not reckon on coming face to face with a large lorry and with no other person at the wheel but Claude's dad who was not known to be one of the most careful drivers around. To avoid a head-on crash, Claude swerved away sharply causing the car to roll over twice in an open field of potatoes. By some miracle, it landed on its wheels and by some stroke of luck, we were not hurt considering that we were bouncing around for a few seconds. The worst thing that happened was that the once grey-coloured car had now taken on a new colour - green, from the foliage of the potato plant.

Claude's dad stepped down from the lorry now about four yards into the canes on the other side. We eventually emerged from the car and stood speechless and motionless in a field of potatoes, our minds drifting between disbelief and despair. The aggressive glare of Claude's dad, whose face was now pumped up with blood, seemed to cast a reddish glow over everything around us. There we stood, our bodies vibrating with fear, in full fire of an outburst of anger that appeared to rock the ground beneath us with every word that shot from his mouth. So thunderous was the outburst that blackbirds in a nearby field took to hasty flight. We said nothing. At no time was Claude told he should not have taken the car without someone knowing. Instead, he was severely scolded for driving off his side. With our combined strength the car was manoeuvred out of the open field and soon we were on our way again. The story reached the village probably before us and for some time was the topic of conversation and the centre of amusement. In a strange way, neither my parents nor Lester's ever got to know about the incident. As we drove home we couldn't help thinking about what could have been the likely alternative outcome: perhaps an ugly mass of metal and flesh.

23

Leader Of The Pack

$\mathcal{J}$ was seventeen, she was fifteen and the second last daughter of the head teacher of St Simons Village School. Her green to grey eyes and attractive smile placed her next to Venus for it was a smile that compelled my emotions to gravitate toward her. Although she lived just up the hill from me, my nearest encounter with Greta was on those rare occasions when she would pass with one or two of her older sisters on their way to visit a family friend in the village or when accompanying her parents to church on Sundays. It was usually a fleeting glance but enough to stimulate the emotions of a young lad.

The talk around the village was about the coming dance for never before was a dance held in the village. It would be the first and it would be held in the village school to raise funds with which to purchase prizes for the speech and prize-giving day that year. The coming event created great excitement among children and adults although everyone was anxious to know what made the vicar give consent to having a dance in the school building.

It was common knowledge that the church would hardly entertain the idea of a dance taking place in any of their school buildings.

Dean Alleyne

It was during that period when the Anglican Church had total control of most primary schools in Barbados. The local vicar hired and fired teachers as well as decided what went on in the school building and dancing was not at the top of the list. We could only assume that permission was granted on the grounds that it was in the interest of the school.

It was dark, about 6:30 pm when the headlights of two cars pierced the darkness. Night falls very quickly in the Tropics. "Those cars are carrying the band," declared Elliot while hastening to finish dressing.

"How do you know that Elliot, it is dark?" I piped up.

"He is like you who think you know everything just because you are going to the Alleyne School," interrupted Calvin my oldest brother who always found it difficult to accept that he himself didn't know everything. Until then, I had not detected what seemed to be a particular dislike of me. It was much later that I found out it was a measure of jealousy which would raise its ugly head from time to time. On one occasion he even referred to me as an educated idiot and I was only in the second year at the Alleyne School. It was an attitude I found difficult to understand since he was given an opportunity of getting a secondary education long before I came on the scene but had blown it.

"It is Stanley Green's band," added Elliot with an expression of confidence. It was a well-known and perhaps the most popular of all the bands in the island and he had often seen and heard it play at other dances before. It wasn't long before we could hear men and women, boys and girls chatting and making their way up the hill to the school. Elliot and Calvin went on ahead with their friends followed by a trail of fragrance from a cocktail of colognes. Frank and I waited for our friends Adrian, George,

John, Errol and Claude. Making our way up the hill we talked about what we were looking forward to doing on the dance floor which included how we would approach those girls with whom we wanted to dance. The difference however between them and me was that I wanted to dance with the head teacher's daughter even though I kept asking myself, *"Will I have the courage to ask her for a dance in the presence of her parents and older brothers and sisters?"* Yet the whole idea gave me a buzz, a ring buzz I mean.

The dark night allowed stars to adorn the night sky in all their beauty and, as we made our way up the hill, we seemed engulfed with balmy air impregnated with the sweet scent of jasmine and lady-of-the-night growing wild in open spaces between houses. Perhaps it was this infusion of fragrances that set my adrenalin alight making me more determined to achieve my objective that night and I could sense that my friends expected me to do so. The school building was ablaze with light from four gas lanterns suspended from the beams, the type you had to pump up before lighting but which when lit, gave off a soft white glow. It is strange how boys tend to suss out what other boys are up to, for they seemed to have caught on to the notion that young adolescent romance was about to germinate between Greta, that attractive green-eyed girl, and me. In some ways, I felt my mother caught wind of it too because she made sure I wore something nice and, like my older brothers, had my hair well-groomed with the pomade of the day all of which only served to reinforce what my friends were thinking.

After spending a little while outside discussing strategy, we crept in and positioned ourselves in a corner, the kind of thing young lads tended to do particularly in the presence of many of their elders. From this vantage point we found delight in watching those on the floor as they expressed their various interpretations of the music. Even the head teacher, whom we never associated with dancing, was doing his bit much to our stifled amusement. But over on the far side was Greta chatting with two of her sisters and I could see clearly that the entire family was there: all five girls and five boys, most of them dancing around the floor. We were all too shy for never before had we danced in public let alone in the presence of our teachers. It was not the 'done thing' but in spite of this psychological barrier, my mind was ablaze with such thoughts as, "*I would like to dance with Greta. I would like to show my friends that I can do it, yes... dance with the prettiest girl in the room. I must rustle up the courage to go over and ask her for a dance*".

This burning desire was reinforced by my friends' eagerness to see me have a go. "Come on Dennis, you can do it," exclaimed Adrian and Claude almost in harmony goading me on, knowing that anything could happen. They really wanted to have a joke at my expense if it went wrong like if I was refused by Greta or told by one of her older brothers or sisters or even by her parents to shove off, in short, if I was snubbed. I could see it becoming a standard joke among my friends for a long time to come. It was at this point however that I remembered one of my mother's sayings: *nothing beats a trial but a failure*. Armed with such a philosophical weapon, I was now ready for the fray. I was now fully pumped up. I could feel the adrenalin racing through my veins while keeping my eyes focused on her.

In the spaces between the gyrating bodies I could see Greta was expecting me to make my way across the floor. By now I realised my friends had lost the courage to approach any of the young damsels and had given up the chase and instead, were quite happy jogging around the floor while keeping a sharp eye on my movements. As for me, I had my target in sight, my Venus. I was now a lad on a mission. My heart stepped up a beat. My body temperature rose sharply. With my mother's saying fixed firmly in the forefront of my mind, I rustled up the kind of courage that propelled me across the floor weaving between dancers to reach Greta in the middle of a calypso I liked very much and which acted as a starting gun for me. I could see she also like the calypso because she was making a slight movement. I was greeted with a smile which did not go unnoticed by her oldest sister standing next to her. It was as though Greta expected me because her hands met mine as I was asking her politely for a dance. Her sister looked over her shoulder and smiled with approval as we set out across the floor demonstrating our own choreographic interpretation of the music much to the amazement of my friends. This was of course accompanied with laughter, her large green eyes taking in the entire scene. Never before had I come so closely to a girl that completely filled my brain. As we continued to dance every tune, I would occasionally glance around to see her brothers looking over at us with an expression which seemed to say, "*It is nice that she is dancing with someone instead of just standing there like a wallflower.*" I was on top of the world that night. In fact, I was so taken up with my dancing that I failed to see my friends had melted away. My courage and success that night pushed me further up the scale in their eyes for I was now seen as leader of the pack.

24

The World Of Work

With my stay at Harrison College completed, I was now about to enter a new phase of development in my life - the world of work. It was customary for former students of the Alleyne School to revisit the school to say hello to staff and share some of their experiences with students. I was adjusting my tie in the mirror before leaving to do just that. My mother was sitting in the rocker by the window showing all the signs of siesta time. Toby the cat, who always seized the opportunity to snooze at this time of the day, jumped onto her lap and made himself comfortable. Mother looked me up and down as if evaluating my outfit before standing to adjust my tie slightly. This provided the perfect opportunity for me to ask her a very delicate question about something that was abiding in my mind for some time. I was about to put on my school blazer but instead opted to sit in the chair beside her.

"Mother, I wanted to ask you something for quite some time now." My eyes narrowed as I spoke with a look of curiosity.

"What is it son?" she asked, rocking very gently and with a look and voice that signalled she too wanted to say something of

Dean Alleyne

great significance. Maybe it was the tranquillity of a hot afternoon causing everything to assume a sluggish appearance that provided a chance for us to think alike. Before I could reply she continued, "You look so grown-up that I think now is the time to tell you something you ought to know because I believe you might be wondering why you were adopted." I drew my chair closer to give her my undivided attention. Just then Toby jumped from her lap to give speedy chase to a house lizard which managed to escape by clambering at full speed up the wall.

"Son, it tore our hearts out to give you away, but with your poor mother losing so many children before six months, we could not refuse the offer of adoption made by such nice people as the Redmans. We always knew you would be in good hands because they had the means to give you the best and I am glad we did. Look at you now. You were brought up in a family with a shop, a big shop too. They even made sure you had a maid to look after you. You were brought up meeting nice people and, most of all my son, they gave you a very good start by putting things in place for you to have a good education, the best that Barbados has to offer." As we looked at each other for a few silent moments, tears that were welling up in her eyes flowed softly down her cheeks like miniature rivulets. She sobbed occasionally blowing her nose as she wiped the tears away. I tried to console her as she continued to tell me what took place on that day when she walked into my adopted parents' shop. I could see we both felt better after that for it was perhaps that final bit that would complete the bond between us.

"But there is something else I have to tell you," she added. I drew my chair even closer to hers and we held each other's hands for I could see that what she was about to say would cause her to relive a painful moment. "Your brother Elliott, who is eight years older than you, had to take at least two or three of your little baby

196

brothers, some still-born, to be buried. Each time he would take the little box on his head early in the morning and put it near the grave for the grave digger to finish the job. The box was no bigger than a shoe box. He would also put the money I gave him for the grave digger under the box.

"Where was my father?" I asked softly.

"Your father would usually be at work by then." As she told me this story I could see she was hurting for I felt some of the pain myself. The thought that immediately gripped my mind was *my poor mother and thank heavens he didn't have to take me.* At the same time, I felt very sorry for my brother. *What an experience for a little boy of no more than eleven or twelve to have!* I thought. Having shared the story with me, a kind of quiet relief crept slowly across her face. We hugged each other for some time, a hug only broken when she felt it was time for me to go. "Have a good afternoon my son." As I started my journey, I momentarily glanced back to see her standing in the doorway waving me on. It all reminded me of when I was setting out for my first day at school in Speightstown for once again, I saw a mother with satisfaction, contentment and pride written all over her face behind a soft smile.

Many of those students I had left in the middle forms were now in the final year and they had remembered me as head-prefect. I was having a chat with a group of small boys in the shade of a large rubber tree the leaves of which displayed shades of green and purple under the intense afternoon sun. Approaching us from the veranda was the current head-prefect who seemed to be on a mission. "Excuse me Dennis' the headmaster would like to see you in his office before you leave." I looked at the messenger and I thought of the person who sent the message and the place to which I was summoned and even then a slight chill crept down my spine, for such a combination of person and room always meant a harrowing experience for me. "Thank you. Please let him know I am just about to finish an interesting conversation with a small group of fourth form boys and that I'll be there in five minutes." The real purpose for the delay was to allow me time to psych up myself to meet the head in that room again. I was soon on my way. I knocked and it was that voice that had often sent shock waves through my body many times before.

"Come in Dennis, it's nice to see you again. How are you?" he said, rising from his chair to shake my hand. After a few very brief pleasantries, he asked to be excused and quickly disappeared to the adjoining room to ask the maid to prepare some light refreshments. This gave me a brief moment to scrutinise the executioner's den. A small bundle of bamboo canes still stood in the corner, the tools of the executioner. There was also a box of chalk sitting on the same small table by the window. On the side opposite the window was a set of shelves carrying his books. On his desk was the usual pile of books for marking. It was the first time I had the chance to look carefully at the room. Other occasions were fleeting and saw me pre-occupied with fear and trembling while focussing on the cane as it went up only to crash onto my backside with such force as to make me see stars rather than anything else in the room. How could I ever forget such moments! On that day too, he was wearing the same white jacket. It was all a brutal reminder of the immeasurable pain I had suffered in the very room and at the hands of the very person in the same white jacket now sitting before me.

"I am keeping well," I replied, levelling my eyes with his as we shook hands, the words leaving my mouth somewhat jerky.

"You *do* look smart," he continued. "You can remove your blazer,"

Walking Through The Pain

"Thank you." I was wearing my full school uniform including the blazer with the school badge firmly positioned on my breast pocket. It was a badge to be proud of. My mother made sure my white shirt was whiter than white which provided just the background for my gold and red tie to stand out. Over pieces of cake and cold ginger-beer, we talked about a number of things. He put his empty glass on the table and cleared his throat.

"Look Dennis, how would you like to teach here for two terms? You see, Mr Brendon is going to England to do a course and I am looking for someone to teach Latin and English. If you did, you could be in line for a permanent post because we are looking to expand from 80 students to 120 in the coming year which means we will require more staff." It took me some time before I could respond for my brain immediately became fired with myriad thoughts. The whole idea took me by storm. Eventually I straightened myself in my chair and signalled my decision with a gentle nod.

"Yes, I would like that very much." I was now feeling more relaxed and composed. He thanked me for not forgetting the school and I thanked him for giving me an opportunity to teach at my old school.

"When you arrive next term, come straight to the staff room." This was a small room next to his office both of which were in his residence adjacent to the school. I would now be joining the staff of three on mornings making that short walk from the staffroom to stand on the platform in the hall for assembly. As I stood there looking into the faces of boys and girls listening to what the head had to say, I could not but recall my days doing a similar thing two years ago. What I did not envisage at the time was that one day I too would be on the platform standing next to a painting of Sir John Gay Alleyne on one side, the founder

199

of the school and one of Queen Elizabeth II on the other. It was a wonderful experience and one I shall never forget. I too found myself sitting in the very chair from which I would often be sentenced to a caning by the head and, like him, I took full advantage of the cooling sea-breeze stealing its way across Long Pond through the east window on those hot afternoons. I enjoyed doing the job and gave it my best shots for I was now looking to the future.

My first pay cheque was for ninety-nine dollars which I gave to my mother as I wasn't too sure what to do with it. She looked at it me with an expression of sheer content and delight.

"This is what I'm going to do. I'm going to ask your uncle Wilbert to look around for a nice young cow, a heifer and buy it for you. Is that alright?"

"Yes, that's okay with me." I trusted her judgement for her advice always proved to be right. Like old Tom, who had the plot of land next to ours near the river, uncle Wilbert also wore dungaree trousers which ended between his knees and ankles and also carried a very sharp knife he used for cutting grass for his animals. He enjoyed working on the land and was a successful small peasant farmer. In fact, he was one of the first to adopt contour farming in the village. It was a method of tilling the soil to run with the contours of the land, a method brought to his attention by the local agricultural administrator at a village meeting. Although the benefits to be gained were pointed out, the only peasant farmer willing to try it was uncle Wilbert who was sometimes laughed to scorn until he was seen to be very successful.

He soon found a young heifer which he bought and handed over to someone who would look after it for half the yield. It was a custom among villagers in rural Barbados whereby every other calf born to the heifer would go to the keeper. It was a verbal agreement but one that worked well. It was the first thing I owned using my funds and it was a great feeling. Very soon my uncle had bought six cows for me. He was in charge of seeing that everything went okay with the keepers and it was a job he took seriously. I had come to the end of my short-term contract at the school and was having a quiet chat with the two other members of staff in the staffroom on the last day of term when the head came in and asked me to come to his office when it was convenient. After the distribution of reports, school was dismissed directly after lunch. Soon eighty boys and girls had melted away in all directions so eager were they to get home early that day. I went to see him as requested.

"I want to thank you for all you have done. You certainly did a good job holding the fort for us in the absence of Mr. Brendon who will be back next term. Come and see me during the holidays and I will tell you how things are going about joining the staff on a permanent basis." This immediately threw my brain into fast rewind. *Why don't I find those words reassuring? Where did I hear them before and what was the outcome? Oh, yes, I had heard it from the very person sitting in front of me, the very person who had promised to arrange my transfer to Harrison College. What makes me now think he will honour his word this time?* I suddenly snapped out of this mental reverse mode to find his hand ready to receive mine in a shake.

"Thank you very much and I will see you during the summer holidays," I replied, looking at him trying to wear a convincing mask of sincerity. I wanted to feel I was on the threshold of something good but hurtful memories of what had happened before were seeping through my veins. *"Why would this be any different?"* I pondered.

Dean Alleyne

During the holidays I went to see him as requested on three occasions none of which proved to be positive. He could never give me any news about what to do next or what to expect. I soon realised that he was merely playing the *delaying tactics* card for I could see the extension to the building going up and fast approaching completion and my hope was fading. The building was completed and the new term had started and I had not even been told about the outcome of our discussions. The staff was significantly increased but I was not even given an interview. I felt humiliated and disappointed. With my hopes now completely dashed, I was a broken person. To me, there was only one thing left to be done which was not in keeping with my character.

It was the last weekend of the summer break and it was a Sunday morning when I got on my bicycle and made my way to the headmaster's residence. I knew he would be at home because he was not a church-goer and he usually watered his roses around mid-morning on Sundays. This he was doing when I arrived. Red, white and yellow roses as well as ginger lilies displayed a mosaic of colour under a mid-morning tropical sunshine which also seemed to arouse a cocktail of breath-taking aroma. Hearing the bike approaching on the gravel surface, he turned to find me carefully leaning it against his steps. I had the feeling he recognised it was not going to be a pleasant meeting and I was right for in less than ten minutes all hell broke loose. The explosive dialogue that followed brought his maid rushing to the nearest window to witness the drama. It was one that saw words exchanged like rapid gunfire. They were penetrating and loud. That done, he returned to his roses and I to my bike. This time no pleasantries were exchanged on arrival or departure. One could cut this section of the atmosphere with an axe. Within ten minutes of leaving, I was on the steps of the Rectory, the home of the parish Vicar who was at that time the chairman of the governing body for the Alleyne School and who had a persuasive say in appointments. Here too I voiced my feelings in no uncertain terms. Dressed in a white long robe and standing tall at the top of the steps, he looked down at me with a degree of contempt and disdain.

"You know, if this was the previous rector, he would have called the police for you." I looked up at him with an aggressive glare.

"I don't care what you do. Do whatever you like." I don't think he quite expected the response I gave him but, having given vent to my feelings, I got on my bike and slowly made my way home. As I pushed the bike slowly up the long hill home in the noonday sun, I had time to reflect on what I had done. I thought of Elliott, the brother who always stood by me. At that time, in addition to his job at the sugar factory, he was the rector's official chauffeur and general assistant at the rectory and the church for he had been taught to drive by the rector. I felt I had to tell him because I pondered the likely repercussions it might have for him and how he would react to me.

"I feel the headmaster could have at least called you in and let you know the position instead of keeping you dangling so to speak at the end of a rope. That way you would have been able to make alternative arrangements. Now here you are at the start of a new term without a job. You were just used to stop a hole but don't worry about it Dennis," he said calmly. We never spoke anymore about it. After that I was so distraught that I became disinterested in work of any kind. Instead, I spent the next four months just chatting around with boys from the village or playing dominoes all day under a tree by the side of the road. They did not have a secondary education but I found it a pleasure and very gratifying to indulge in conversations covering a variety of topics ranging from who planted what in their plots to local and

Dean Alleyne

national politics. Gone were the days of just wandering around with my younger friends. My new friends were now much older and were all skilled or manual workers who were glad to have me around for a while at least.

25

Getting To Grips With Primary-School Teaching

*D*uring the four months that went by I thoroughly enjoyed myself in the company of my newly-found friends. It was probably a way of re-charging my batteries. I had no desire to become a primary school teacher preferring instead to teach at secondary level. I had faced disappointments during my school career and had overcome them with the help of my mother and brother but I had just experienced my first set back in the world of work. However, it soon became clear to me that, if I was to move on in a country with a narrow based economy, I would have to rethink the way I was going about things. It was time for *biting the bullet,* for making an apology to the parish rector who controlled the primary schools in St Andrew. It was he who could recommend me to the Department of Education for a teaching post in the parish. This I did and was offered an acting post at a small primary school in Bawdens, a small village about four miles from St Simon's as the crow flies. It was a school of no more than about 120 boys staffed by four teachers including the head teacher.

Dean Alleyne

Like St Simon's, Bawdens Village also stood on a low hill from which the land dipped very gently on three sides. Here a few families grew a mixture of sugar cane, bananas, cassava, yams, peppers, peas, beans and other short crops, a kind of subsistence farming. In some ways, with its one small shop and no more than twelve houses, it seemed cut off from the rest of the parish. I couldn't help thinking I was stationed there as a kind of punishment for giving vent to my feelings that Sunday morning in the presence of the rector. But it was at this school that I learned the basic principles of teaching, principles that stood the test of time throughout my teaching career. The head teacher was short, a bit corpulent and very dark and, like most head teachers of the time, a disciplinarian. He always wore braces to support his trousers around his rotund waist. I often felt his strength was in teaching choral singing to the entire school on Friday afternoons. It seemed as though this was where most head teachers of primary schools excelled. It was a way of giving staff time to get their attendance registers in order and prepare lessons for the following week.

My method of getting to work was by pedal-bike using a back route along narrow tracts up and down slopes, some with large boulders in the way but it was a shorter way than that along the main road. However, if it rained, I took the longer but safer route along the main road through Belleplaine. What was certain is that both routes meant an uphill grind in a very hot post three o'clock sun which sapped one's energy. I would arrive home in the late afternoon with my shirt completely soaked though with perspiration. It was a Friday the last day of term when I reached home around 4 o'clock exhausted and wet through and through after pushing my bike uphill for more than two miles in a blazing afternoon sun. As I leaned it against the house, I turned to find my mother gazing at me with a pensive look.

Walking Through The Pain

"Dennis, why don't you sell a couple of the cows and buy a motorcycle? You can then go further than just to school. You'll be able to visit some of our family and you won't be sweaty. Ask Elliot to help you find a good one." She had obviously seen my plight and, as usual, had given a lot of thought as to the best alternative to get to work.

"What a good idea," I replied removing my lunch bag from the handle of my bike. Until then, I had never given it a thought. However, within a few days, I got in touch with Elliott who was then married and living far away from home. He already had a motorcycle which he shared with Calvin and, as usual, he too was glad to help.

"I know where I can get a very good second-hand one in town. I know because sometimes I go there and have a look around. We can go on Saturday and have a look together," he suggested. In the meantime, mother had wasted no time in alerting uncle Wilbert about converting two of my cows into money. Within two weeks we had purchased the motorcycle and, with my brother's tuition, I was soon mastering the skills of riding. Yes, I was now getting to work and back feeling fresh, but I was also able to take my nocturnal meanderings further afield and to join other friends on excursions and picnics to any part of the island, be it day or night. To have a motorcycle that looked almost new was not only of utility value to the user but a kind of social magnet attracting the attention of girls who tended to gravitate toward the rider. Nothing felt more gratifying to me than having a girl of my choice riding pinion and with that fresh tropical breeze rushing pass our faces. Picnics, beach parties and the cinemas were favourite haunts where fellow riders would also meet and chat about their adventures.

After successfully completing one year at Bawdens Primary

School, I was given a permanent post at St John the Baptist Primary, a much larger school with well over three hundred pupils situated in Holders Hill, St James and within easy reach of Holetown on the west coast. It was customary in those days to appoint a young teacher as far away from home as possible on their first permanent post. I never knew why. This is where the motorcycle proved invaluable because there was no cross country bus between St Simons and Holetown. I received a warm welcome from the head-teacher who was introducing me to members of staff individually when I heard a muffled call from behind. "Hello Dennis, nice to see you. So you are the new member of staff we were expecting!" It was the voice of Alvin my favourite teacher from St Simon's Village School, the very teacher who first stimulated my interest in geography. He was thrilled to see one of his former students now becoming a teaching colleague of his.

"What a pleasant surprise, how long have you been here?" I asked while shaking hands with broad smiles all around. The head teacher looked at us with mild astonishment.

"It seems as though you two know each other, so I'll leave you to it," he interjected before wandering off to prepare for morning assembly. My first impression of the head teacher was that he was quite pleasant and more informed than the head at Bawdens Primary School which proved to be true.

"I joined the staff about three years ago," replied Alvin. "I applied for a school nearer home and was posted here. It is quite near to where I live in Arch Hall," he added. My stay at St John the Baptist School though short was enjoyable if only for two things. First Alvin, my former teacher and now colleague, was extremely good in helping me to settle into my new surroundings and, in a way, became my mentor. Secondly, he too rode a motor cycle to school so we had a lot in common we could talk about. "After school I'll like to show you around," he suggested. That afternoon we rode down to Paynes Bay and took a quiet stroll on the beach where he pointed out the monument and the plaque in Holetown showing that the British first landed here on the island in 1625 and named the settlement Jamestown after its benefactor James 1st of England. Its name was afterward changed to Holetown because here ships would dock in the small harbour to be cleaned up.

After dinner that day my mother and I were having a quiet chat. She gazed at me with a feeling of satisfaction. "I am proud of you my son. You must always try to do your best at work like you did at school. By the way, we have relatives in Paynes Bay whom you don't know but I will tell you where they live and you can drop in to say hello. I am sure they'll be glad to know you." The following afternoon I took a similar trip to Paynes Bay less than a mile away as I was anxious to find my relatives. I had just parked my bike under a coconut tree when I noticed less than fifty yards away along the beach a small group of women with large baskets looking out to sea. My attention alternated between the boats coming in with their catch and the women gazing eagerly out to sea. There were awaiting the arrival of a flotilla of small fishing boats with their white sails bobbing up-and-down between the waves as they made their way to shore. Just then one of the women left the group and made her way slowly to me. She looked at me with an inquiring but cautious expression. Obviously there was something about me that attracted her attention.

"Are you the new teacher at St John the Baptist School just up the hill?

"Yes," I replied, anxiously awaiting the next question.

"Someone told me you are from St Simon's Village. Is that so?" she asked, levelling her eyes with mine.

"Yes," I replied.

"Is your mother's name, Alice?" I nodded in agreement to both questions whereupon she came close and gave me a big hug. She was thrilled and pointed out that she was a cousin of my mother and that she lived less than three hundred yards from the beach. "Can you see the second-last boat in that group over there?" she asked, pointing to the small flotilla.

"Yes," I replied, returning my focus on the flotilla.

"That is my husband's and I am waiting for his catch," she added. "I know you have never met him so I'll introduce you to him when he comes in." Once beached with the help of other volunteers, he was about to leave the catch to his wife to be sold directly from the boat to women with large trays and baskets who would in turn sell them to their customers in the surrounding area. He was at sea most of the night but tired and sleepy as he was, she managed a brief introduction.

Albert her husband was a direct descendant of the poor white community and as such had missed out on a secondary education. In fact, I wasn't too sure he even had an elementary education. In spite of this he was very pleasant and hard-working and, like other fishermen, the stress of being alone at sea all night in a tiny boat could clearly be seen on his furrowed face and dishevelled hair. He too wore trousers which reached just below his knees and, more often than not, were torn in places. He would leave the boat carrying his lantern, his coal pot and the remainder of his food in a container. It was a busy time of the afternoon with buyers making bids on quantities of fish of which there was a variety. I was often given a supply of flying fish, king fish, snapper, mullet, or shark to take home twice per week. It was always a pleasure to join fisherwomen standing on the sandy beach watching the little boats come in with their catch and with the afternoon sun beating down on the water with such intensity as to make it almost impossible to look out to sea due to the glare. Such pleasure was brought to an abrupt end one afternoon by an incident which by a twist of fortune saw me catapulted back to my village school to teach.

I had just collected my usual supply of fish and, having strapped the bag onto the handle of the bike, I started to pull away but, on attempting to straighten up, the bike refused to respond. In fact, I found myself shunted speedily to the other side of the road. In a way I was very lucky for there was no oncoming traffic. It was the sheer speed of moving off that saw me heading for a deep roadside ditch on a bike that seemed totally out of control. It was as though the bike had a mind of its own for, within seconds, I landed head first in a deep roadside ditch, the bike on top of me still rumbling away. There was no shortage of helpers to retrieve me and my bike. This unfortunate incident came about because of a change of bikes. For some reason my brother and I decided we would swap bikes that day. My bike was the type with a back stand suspending the back wheel when parked, an Ariel. It meant that when you move off, the stand would automatically flip up at the back without your assistance. My brother's carried a side stand, a Triumph, which required you to kick it up before you could go. I moved off as usual unmindful of the side stand which dictated where I ended up...in the ditch about five feet deep.

"There is a lot of blood on your shirt," shouted someone from the small crowd that had gathered. I looked to find that my once white shirt was now one-third covered with blood around my

Dean Alleyne

left arm. I had not realised I had sustained a deep gash from a jagged tree stump as I was thrown into the ditch. I was soon taken to my relatives not far away to await Elliot who soon arrived and wasted no time getting me to the nearest doctor who cleaned and stitched the wound without anything to reduce the pain. Soon, riding pinion with my brother, I was home with my arm strapped. I was off from school for about three weeks when it dawned on me that it was an opportune moment to apply for a school nearer to my home, my village school for instance. I had hoped that my accident would be seen as grounds for mitigating circumstances.

Having served two terms at St John the Baptist Primary School I applied and, to my surprise, was given a transfer to St Simon's Village School even before the end of my sick leave. So quickly did events unfold that I did not even get the chance to say goodbye to the staff. I was now within walking distance of work and no need for a bike during the day. This afforded my younger brother Frank a chance to learn to ride during the day. So here I was again about to teach at the same school which gave me such a torrid welcome about twelve years before. I showed my mother the letter confirming my appointment at the village school. She was delighted. "I know we will miss our regular supply of fish from my cousin but you will be able to have lunch with me every day," she declared.

That said, her facial expression took on a slightly sombre mood. "You don't know this but Elliot was sent by the vicar to teach at St Simons about five years ago. He had noted his progress through school and had concluded that he had the ability to do the job and that, with training he could make a success of it, but the head teacher and some of the teachers gave him so much hell that he had to give it up after only one term," she exclaimed.

Walking Through The Pain

"But why did they do such a thing?" I asked in sheer disgust.

"I suppose they didn't think a local lad from a humble background whose parents could not afford him shoes to wear to school, ought to be given a chance to improve himself."

"Do you know who was responsible for this?" I asked forcefully for I was now becoming a bit heated under the collar.

"Believe me when I tell you it was the same teacher that wanted to prevent you from going to the Alleyne School." Elliot had never received a secondary education but then neither did those teaching at the school except for one, the very teacher who eventually became my favourite teacher at St Simons and whom I had later met at St John the Baptist Primary School. He had attended the Alleyne School and had done very well and, as it happened, he also turned out to be Elliot's favourite teacher. Except for him, all the others, including the one who caned me on my very first day managed to convince the head that Elliot ought to be removed.

I thanked my mother very much for it galvanised my determination not to let that happen to me because I knew I was more qualified than any of them bar one. This transfer to my own village school meant that I was able to take a short walk home for lunch, less than one hundred and fifty yards. It was an occasion for my mother and me to chat about this and that over lunch. I was having a cold drink on this occasion when, in glancing at the clock, my eyes caught a photo of Calvin. I had seen it every day but this time it triggered a thought which was abiding with me for a long time. I slowly placed my glass on the table while giving my mother a side glance.

"Mother, why is it that Calvin never came to see me when I was a

213

kid in Speightstown and he never seems interested in what I am doing?" My brow was furrowed as I asked the question although I took care not to put any pressure on her for an answer. She took off her hat and fanned her face while making her way to the rocking chair. With twenty-five minutes to the end of lunch-time, I drew up a chair to listen.

"Dennis, I tried several times to get him to go to Speightstown to see you but he just wouldn't go. He always found an excuse." I nodded slowly.

"Why do you think he was like that toward me, after all I was only a little kid?" She placed her head firmly on the back of the rocker.

"For some reason, I don't think he ever liked you," she replied looking as though she was apologising for him but, with only ten minutes remaining, I had just enough time to return to school.

As part of my probation, I had to be observed by one of the two chief inspectors of schools. The topic I selected to teach a class of nine-year olds that day was '*the use of adjectives*'. This required visual aids, not the kind of resources easily obtainable at that time. I had therefore spent some time preparing my own a few days before. The inspector arrived and, after a brief chat with the head teacher, was shown to my class. Introductions were brief.

"What lesson are you teaching today?" The question came in a manner that was non-threatening, one that relaxed me immediately.

"This is class 2 and I want to teach them a little bit about adjectives and how they are used. I aim to keep it as simple as possible."

"I see you have some visual aids," he continued, quickly shuffling through a few sheets of paintings on my table. "Did you prepare them yourself?" he asked raising his head with a smile. I took this to mean I was off to a very good start.

"Oh yes Sir," I replied, with chalk in my hand and now anxious to get started.

"Okay, when you are ready" he said, and made his way to a seat at the back of the class.

Just then I took a quick glance through the nearest east window as though appealing to the deities for that extra help. Tops of sugar cane in a nearby field were making waves under the effect of a welcoming breeze that seemed to blow away any nervousness I might have had. 'Discipline' was never a problem in schools in those days which meant that the teaching situation could take place. The lesson was a resounding success. In fact, so spellbound was the inspector, that for a moment I had the feeling he had never before seen the topic put over in that manner to a class of nine-year olds. I had in effect now passed my probation. He congratulated me and, after another brief chat with the head teacher, was soon on his way back to Bridgetown. What was blatant however, was that none of the teachers came over to congratulate me but by then I was too elated with joy anyway to pay much attention to that.

26

Distant Horizons

After two years at St Simon's Village School my burning desire to teach in a secondary school had not faded. The six-months stint at the Alleyne Secondary School had convinced me that I could make a success of teaching at secondary level. The opportunity came with the appointment of a new vicar to the Anglican Church in St Simon's. He had just finished his usual Wednesday morning service at the village school which became necessary during the building of a new church. It was now morning break and he was having a chat with some members of staff while I was sitting at my desk preparing a lesson when my concentration was broken by unusual heavy footsteps behind me. I turned and, approaching me with a hand already in the shaking position was the vicar, a tall well-built man under a full-length black robe and a pair of thin metal-framed glasses. It was the kind of greeting that was already making him very popular in the village, a single expression of a character compelling you to gravitate toward him. He leaned forward slowly as though not wanting others to hear what he was about to say.

"Would you like to teach at the Coleridge & Parry School?" he whispered. For once I was lost for words. A number of thoughts crowded my mind within seconds. *"Could this be the beginning of another chapter in my life?"* I stood still stringing out the moment. I knew what my response would be but I couldn't believe what I had just heard. My eyes reached passed him to gaze at a rainbow softly hugging the hills in the distance and caressing the very pastures where, as boys, we tethered our small flock of sheep. It was the relics of a mid-morning shower. It was the bell to signal the end of morning break that interrupted my focus in time for me to recognize his hand was still in the shaking position.

"Yes, I would like that very much." *Is this my lucky day? Is this really true?* Were some of the thoughts that engulfed my mind as I drifted between disbelief and excitement.

"Good, I'll give you a letter to take to the headmaster." He immediately returned to the head teacher's desk where he wrote a short letter to the headmaster of Coleridge & Parry Secondary School. "Make sure you take this to the headmaster no later than Sunday." I thanked him very much. I was given a second chance by a person who knew very little about me but whose very character exuded sincerity. I later worked out that he had gathered much of his information about me from Elliot who became as close to him as he was to the former vicar. He had obviously told him about the hurdles which I had to jump over to reach where I was and that they had never deterred me.

Coleridge & Parry School was larger than the Alleyne School and was located in the parish of St Peter adjacent to St Andrew, but there was no cross-country bus connection. At lunch I told my mother the good news. "Remember what I said, *time is longer than twine*? You must tell your father and Elliot this evening. I'm sure they will be glad to hear the good news." Her face glowed with delight. On hearing the news, Elliot laughed. He was not at all surprised for he had grown very close to the village vicar whom he had kept updated with my progress in teaching so far.

"Have you noticed that this appointment is also on a Sunday afternoon? Let us hope you'll be as successful with this as you were when we went to see the headmaster at Harrison College," declared Elliot. Although I had my motorcycle, my parents insisted that we should get a car for this trip. Elliot had become a good friend of the organist at St Simon's Church who was teaching him to play the organ. Indeed, he would even come to us on occasions for Sunday lunch and had often lent Elliot his car - a Vauxhall - to run errands for the vicar or to take guests to weddings. Getting the car for the trip to see the headmaster of the Coleridge & Parry School was therefore not a problem. That Sunday, I delivered the letter and was interviewed and offered the job which I accepted. I would now be teaching Latin and Geography from September, the start of the new term and academic year. The news brought unbridled joy from my parents and the rest of the family who were thrilled to know that I had at last landed a permanent post at a secondary school and none more so than my aunt Ersil, my favourite aunt, who was on holiday from Curacao and had visited us for Sunday dinner.

Ersil lived in Curacao where she worked as a bank clerk. She was younger than my mother and very attractive and had obviously been very successful. This was noticed in the way she dressed: a stylishly cut dress supported on tall heels, earrings and a matching necklace that settled elegantly on her bosom. She was taller than my mother and spoke with a measure of confidence. As she sat cross-legged on my father's favourite chair by the window enjoying the late afternoon breeze, I could see from her contented expression that she had been brought up to date with my career and that, like my parents, she was also eagerly awaiting news of my interview. After hearing the news and joining in the celebration, she took two sips of a rum punch made by Elliot and rested her glass on the table before turning to me with that soft familiar smile reminiscent of her visits to me as a kid in Speightstown.

"But *how* are you going to get there because it is a good distance away and there is no bus running from here to Speightstown?" At that time all bus routes converged on Bridgetown. There was no cross-country service and my aunt was well aware of that, although I couldn't quite understand why she had asked that question knowing I already had a motorcycle which I thought would do the job. She had a different agenda. "But by the way, where is Calvin? He ought to be here on an occasion like this to congratulate Dennis for all his achievements," she uttered looking rather surprised. Elliot cleared his throat.

"I can never understand why he treats Dennis like that. He never seems to be interested in anything he does. You may not know this auntie but when Dennis was going to the Alleyne School most of his friends cycled to school. Dad had a bike he wasn't using but it wanted some repairs done to it. Calvin was good at that but neither my dad nor mum could get him to get the bike ready for Dennis. In fact, he took it to pieces and never re-assembled it again. The excuse he always gave was that he was too busy so Dennis therefore had to walk the four miles to and from school in the scorching sun every day for five years carrying a bag of books." This shook auntie whose face suddenly assumed a serious expression. It was not the kind of thing she expected from an older brother. "I can only assume he feels Dennis should not be back here after enjoying the kind of life he himself never had and even though he had an opportunity to have a secondary education which he messed up. He now seems to be jealous over Dennis having the chance to go to the Alleyne School and Harrison College," exclaimed Elliot.

"I will use my motorcycle," I replied, looking at Elliot and my mother who were as puzzled as me on hearing the question my aunt had asked.

"Oh no," she said. She had now become more adamant to give all the help she could after hearing what Elliot had to say. "You are not doing anything such thing. It is too dangerous to ride that distance and what happens when it rains?" Dad and mother looked at each other. I looked at auntie who had momentarily slipped into pensive mood. Nothing was said for a few seconds. The only thing that stirred was the side of the oilskin table cloth disturbed by a light breeze creeping stealthily through the window pass the large jug that kept water cool. We anxiously awaited auntie's next words. Dad reached across the table and topped up her glass to which she added some Coca Cola. She adjusted the pendant on her necklace which seemed to flicker with every move she made.

"I want you and Elliot to go to town next Saturday and look at those cars in Courtesy Garage. Choose the one you like and let me know," she said breezily with her eyes moving between Elliot and me. Courtesy Garage was one of three dealers in Barbados for new and used cars. Smiles of expectation crept across our faces. We looked at each other without questioning what she said. After all, she was my mother's favourite sister and my favourite aunt. She was the one who visited me most of all my aunts when I was just a kid in Speightstown. Elliot was in the midst of finishing off a chicken leg but he paused for a moment.

"Yes auntie, we'll go to town next Saturday and have a look, I'm sure we will find something," uttered Elliot, before returning to the job of the chicken leg.

"Now you make sure you choose something nice," she added.

At the car dealer's that Saturday we looked around for a while before settling on a used Hillman, a bit the worse for wear, but one which we thought would do the job, or at least that is what Elliot thought. The following Sunday, auntie again joined us for dinner. Dad had got himself a nice leg of lamb from the village butcher that morning for it was customary for the village butcher to slaughter an animal on Sunday mornings and immediately sell it to waiting customers, meat being the thing you ate only on Sundays. On other days, it was usually fresh fish bought from vendors carrying trays or baskets on their heads laden with freshly caught fish from the sea. The alternative was usually tined fish, corned beef or salted cod. Auntie held the topic back until after dinner when, with her favourite drink in her hand, she looked at Elliot and me almost simultaneously. "Well my boys, did you see anything you liked?"

"Yes auntie. We saw a second-hand Hillman we like....," piped up Elliott expecting her approval, but before he could give his description and opinion of what we had seen, auntie interjected under a frowned forehead.

"Oh no! no! not that one. Oh no. I want you to go back next Saturday and you'll see a car in the right hand corner. I am sure you will like it," she uttered with that usual air of confidence. This left us even more puzzled for we had seen a car in the corner of the showroom as she indicated but never thought she would think of buying a new car for me. On our return to the dealer, there it was, a light grey Vauxhall Victor with the chrome so bright that it dazzled in the noonday sun penetrating the large glass window. It was one of a small range of modern cars to hit the island in the early 60s. We were looking around the car discussing whether it was the one she was talking about when I heard footsteps. I turned sharply to see a young well-dressed salesman coming toward us with a facial expression that said *these two chaps look like possible buyers.* Before I could alert Elliott, the all too customary question was emerging slowly from the salesman's lips: "What can I do for you gentlemen, have you seen anything you like?" Without looking at the salesman and keeping his eyes fixed on the Vauxhall, Elliott replied, "We like this car but I wonder if this is the one our aunt has asked us to look at."

"Oh dear, you will have to choose another one because a woman came in two days ago, paid for it and asked us to hold it until Saturday, that is today." We looked at each other wondering if we were on the right track. "What did she look like?" I asked, as though expecting him to say what I wanted to hear. "She was well-dressed and spoke like someone from down the islands, you know, Trinidad for instance." My aunt had spent some time in Trinidad before moving on to Curacao. Our minds were racing. *"Could that person be auntie and could this be the car she meant?"* We pondered between ourselves for a moment. But while in this pensive and somewhat perplexed mood, Elliott came across what he thought was a clue.

"Look Dennis, it has a St Andrew number plate." We looked at each other again in wonderment before Elliot turned to the salesman. "Can you tell us the name of the person who bought this car?" he asked anxiously. "Just hold on a minute." He dashed off to his office in search of the paper. "Come over here," he said fingering through a couple of files. "Ah here it is. Her name is Ersil and she lives in Curacao." We both broke into a smile that became an extended chuckle of delight for we had made the right choice. It was soon clear that auntie had done a lot of work unknown to us. Having told the salesman the whole story and satisfied him that we were her relatives, we were handed the keys. Soon we were on our way to St Simon's with Elliott at the wheel. The views we passed never looked more beautiful; the

Dean Alleyne

breeze floating through the windows never felt more soothing and the smell of new upholstery never more satisfying than on that first drive from Bridgetown to St Simon's in a new Vauxhall Victor.

To have a motorcycle was one thing but to arrive in the village with a new car at the age of twenty was something totally different. Elliot drove slowly through the village as though he wanted everyone to know this was our new car. He was not disappointed because it wasn't long before we were followed by a group of youngsters trying to keep pace. It was something resembling the Pied Piper of Hamlin and his followers. Once parked in the shade of a tree near the house, it underwent a thorough inspection by the pursuing group including adults, each member seeking to demonstrate their knowledge of this type of car. As Elliot removed the keys, I looked around and there was my mother enjoying the theatre from a window. Her expression said it all, *I am very proud of you my boys.*

The start of the new term at Coleridge & Parry was only eight weeks away. Elliot thought it was enough time to give me a crash course in learning to drive. The tuition was intense for he stopped at nothing to ensure I reached the required standard. One of the lessons took us pass the open gates of a village school in St Joseph. "Stop the car. Let's change places." I went through the procedure for stopping a vehicle safely. He took the wheel. "This is something the police inspector will ask you to do, so watch what I do carefully." I gave it my undivided attention as he reversed the car between the two pillars from both sides three times while describing what he was doing and why. "Now I want you to do exactly what I just did." After a few attempts I was soon mastering the manoeuvre much to his delight. This was followed by a manoeuvre whereby I had to stop the vehicle on a steep hill and move off again without the vehicle rolling back

224

even one centimetre. But there was one last tricky manoeuvre still to come. I was asked to stop the car at the bottom of a hill at the top of which was a bend. He looked at the hill and at me as though to say *let's see if he can do this without my showing him how to do it.* "Now I want you to reverse the car up the hill and around the bend at the top without stopping." This I did once, twice, three times with relative ease. "Okay, I think you are ready for the test. I'll get a date set for next week because I can't see you having any problem." It gave me a great feeling to know he had so much confidence in his younger brother.

It was a busy weekday when we set off to the testing station. Testing was conducted by an inspector of police who would first ask you a few simple questions on the road code before putting you on the road. The inspector I had was known to be the most vigilant and ruthless of the traffic cops with a facial expression so hard and chiselled as to strike fear in you. He was a man whom most drivers dreaded for he was merciless with those caught breaking the speed limit and could often be seen waiting around corners or hiding in tall grass by the roadside awaiting his next victim. Questions and answers over, we were ready for the road. In a strange way, I had no fear. Instead I felt rather confident. "I want you to go through those gates, stop and then reverse through the gate from the left and then from the right." This I did flawlessly with the inspector and Elliot standing just inside the gate. I could sense my brother was quite pleased with how things had gone so far.

We boarded the car, the inspector occupying the front passenger seat. "Now I want you to go through the gates again and turn left, I will tell you what to do from there on." Again I carried out the manoeuvres successfully. From time to time I would also see my brother smiling quietly in the back seat. I felt there was another one to come, a tricky one and, as Elliot said, it would be

Dean Alleyne

on the very hill where he had taught me how to do that particular manoeuvre. I was almost at what I thought was the end of the test when I heard: "I want you to stop at the bottom of the hill in the distance. We will get out of the car and I want you to reverse the car up the hill and around the bend at the top without stopping." This I did even faster than with my brother much to the inspector's surprise. His stern countenance melted just a fraction. "Okay, I am satisfied. Let's go back to the station." I was only a small chap, in fact so small that I had to use a cushion to give me extra height. The fact that I was so young and completed the test with ease prompted the inspector to ask: 'By the way, how long was your little brother here driving?' I never heard my brother's response although his eyes said it all. I did ask him some time later but he never gave me an answer. I now had a license to drive and I drove the car home with the greatest of confidence which was just as well because in less than one week, I would be driving solo.

The day came when I took to the road on my own on the long drive to school. It was just after eight and the sun was already beating down with great intensity on a September morning. My brother had made sure the vehicle was spotless and that the chrome sparkled. My mother made sure my shirt was whiter than white and waved me on as I set out. The crop season had ended three months ago and many fields were brown except where the new growth of young cane shoots displayed a slight hint of green with their leaves fluttering in a gentle morning breeze. It was a tint broken here and there by the bobbing heads of women, some wearing colourful head-ties and others floppy straw-hats, but all bent over and carefully removing every blade of grass or weed from between the young plants with hoes. It was tough work but they all seemed to create a kind of harmony expressed through jokes and chatter on a variety of everyday topics. Such was the theatre that greeted me, one I had seen several times before as a boy on my way to and from school on foot. Now here I was making my first solo drive. It felt strange driving slowly down Haggatts Hill pass old Sampson's house and the street standpipe for which my friends and I as small boys would often make a mad dash to quench our thirst on our way back from the sea.

The sugar factory had long ceased to belch out columns of black smoke for it was the end of the season. The only activity was that of a small group of engineers cleaning and repairing machinery in preparation for the start of the next season in January. It was a feeling touched with pride and satisfaction on seeing my brother waiting at the same spot where he would often give me bus fare and pocket money to get to school. As I approached him slowly, we were already greeting each other with smiles of contentment and delight knowing that together we had shared some of the best and some of the worst of times. After a quick joke he wished me good luck in my new job and waved me on my first solo drive to work. It felt rather strange driving for the first time on my own. It was an eerie feeling. I thought of the days, the weeks, the months and the years I pounded this very route on foot with my bag of books to and from school under a hot sun. At times it was so hot that it sapped every bit of energy almost to the point of melting my brain as I slowly made my way home from school carrying a bag of books up Haggatts Hill.

I was admiring the small boys and girls smartly dressed in their uniforms on their way to school that morning (The Alleyne School) when my attention was suddenly broken by a waving hand. It was Mr. Brendon my favourite teacher on his way to work. I smiled, shook my hand and reinforced it with a short toot of the horn. Mr. Brendon was tall and of average build with a set of teeth so white that, if caught in the sun, could force an onlooker to don a pair of shades. He had a charming personality which, with his poise and deportment, compelled you to seek his company. Woven within such characteristics was a high level of tolerance, the kind that often saw him explain things over and over to make sure you understood. I cannot recall him ever exploding even when I did something silly. Instead, he handled it in a manner that helped me to build self-confidence. He was a true professional.

I continued on my first solo drive through Belleplaine and pass the parish church. Soon I was navigating my way pass Greenland Plantation and up Cleland Hill to the top of the highest of the three natural terraces which go to make up Barbados. I stopped for a moment to look back on the beauty of the Scotland District. From here, there is a commanding view of Belleplaine and the east coast. It was a panoramic view sufficiently compelling to see the makers of the movie, *Island in the Sun,* use it as a backdrop. It wasn't long before I was descending a gentle slope westward into the parish of St Peter. Within another twenty minutes I was at school. It was my first solo drive and one I never forgot. I enjoyed my stay at Coleridge & Parry teaching Latin and Geography. But comfortable as I was in my job, it soon dawned on me that I was teaching the same number of lessons as graduates on the staff but was earning less than half their pay. This highlighted the urgency for me to go abroad and complete a first degree and, after a year in the job, I was ready to leave the post and the island for England.

I would be flying on my birthday. At the airport to see me off were my parents, Elliott and one of my aunts. "Here you are Elliot" handing him the keys, "the car is now yours." It was a small way of saying thanks for so much he had done for me. I made a ninety degrees turn and, standing before me, was the woman who was the driving force, my mother smartly dressed as usual and with eyes focused on mine. I sensed it was an expression of joy and sorrow: joy to see that all her hard work, care and attention had brought the desired rewards; sorrow in that she was once again handing over her son to a different world in the hope that life for him would better. As I held her close to me in that final hug the world stood still for a moment. She dabbed a teardrop from her eye. My father who already had a few drinks with a couple of friends he had met in the bar probably as a way of dealing with the parting, shook my hand firmly and fixed his eyes on mine. "I have given your brothers most of the land but we have given you something no one can ever take from you, the best education provided in Barbados. Now go and build on it my boy for we are all proud of you." In twenty minutes I was making my way with others up the steps to board the aircraft, a BOAC then, now British Airways. Reaching the top of the steps, I glanced back briefly to see them waving me on. It was a moment of mixed feelings for I was now leaving the land of my birth and the island which had cradled me in its arms. I was saying goodbye to the people who were so dear to me and who had brought me to the point where I was now ready to go beyond the horizon. I had walked through the pain.

PS: Within two years of arriving in England I entered the University of London to read Geography before joining the teaching service. I taught at four London secondary schools before becoming a head. After retiring, I successfully completed a Doctorate in Education prior to becoming an education consultant, a life coach and a published author.

CPSIA information can be obtained
at www.ICGtesting.com
Printed in the USA
LVOW11s0641010617
536555LV00001B/7/P